MW01710314

Destiny Delivered

Rosemary Gard

ISBN: 978-1-63491-004-0

Published by BookLocker.com, Inc., Bradenton, Florida, U.S.A.

Printed on acid-free paper.

BookLocker.com, Inc.
2015

First Edition

This book is dedicated to the memory of my parents, Josefina and Tomo Babich, who both came to the United States, though not together, in the early 1900s.

My father never learned to read or write, but he could do math problems in his head faster than I could with paper and pencil. There was nothing he could not build or repair.

Josefina went as far as the 4th grade and did learn to read and write. She faithfully read every newspaper she could get her hands on. Nothing was ever wasted or thrown away. Her motto was "If you don't have to feed it, keep it!"

At my 12th birthday I was considered a woman. My mother wanted my gift to be a sewing machine. I wanted a typewriter. After several loud and heated arguments between my parents, my father bought me a Royal portable typewriter.

Destiny works quietly in our lives, and often we feel we have not gotten what we wish for, or what we feel we deserve. But, in the end, be it Karma or fate…we find our Destiny Delivered.

~ Rosemary Gard

PROLOGUE

Though some Croatians were returning to their homeland in the early 1900s, still others were leaving for America.

Stefan Vladeslav was concerned about the political events taking form in Europe. He had enough money to pack up many of the unsold paintings and antiques in his store, in the hopes of shipping them to America to start a new life there.

The Austro-Hungarian government placed such high taxes on the land that entire families were immigrating to America, leaving the fertile land to be taken over by Hungarians.

The Dalmatian wine growers were also suffering because of the importing of Italian wines, causing an exodus from the Dalmatian wine country.

CHAPTER 1

Zagreb, Croatia - 1913

Damn her! Damn Barbra for leaving me.

These words ran through Stefan's thoughts as if it were a litany.

Handsome Stefan Vladeslav sat at his usual table in the back of his now closed store. He looked out at the packed crates and boxes of artifacts which had been the stock in the store. The crates and boxes were made of raw wood, unvarnished and the smell of wood was strong in the dimly lit room. Tables covered with dust cloths reflected thin shafts of light filtering through the shuttered windows, casting a somewhat sad and gloomy atmosphere in the room.

Years ago the building had been a gambling house with women available upstairs. When Stefan acquired the building, it became a place where beautiful paintings and antiques were sold.

Today at 10 o'clock in the morning he was not dressed, still in his dark maroon morning robe. His blue eyes were troubled. Stefan ran his hand through his uncombed dark brown hair. The touch of grey at his temples added to his good looks, as did his trim mustache.

Stefan had inherited the once gambling house and brothel from Magda, his good friend and companion for a couple years. The artifacts had not been accumulated by Magda, but by her ruthless Turkish business partner, Abuh, who disappeared leaving everything to her.

Spread before him on the table were various newspapers collected for him by the waiters at the International Hotel. Old issues of the London Daily Express, the British Middlesex

Gazette, New York Times, The Sun and the Hrvatska Zastava, a Croatian language paper printed in the US.

Carrying a small tray, Ignatz, the loyal and dedicated servant to Stefan and his family, placed the strong aromatic coffee and warm bread on the table, careful not to interfere with the newspapers.

Stefan never looked up. After nearly five years with him, the small man recognized this brooding mood.

When Stefan, along with his father, came to look over the inheritance, they found Ignatz living in the building, taking care of it waiting for Magda's return. Ignatz had been a poor man and on occasion Magda gave him food and some odd jobs. When Magda escaped the Turk, the building was left shuttered. Homeless Ignatz had found a way in through the back and stayed there becoming the self-appointed care taker. Stefan and his father, Anton, were so impressed at the care the slender, five foot Ignatz provided while the building was closed, they hired him to stay on and work for them.

Now, he was part of the family. A family that once was made up of Stefan, his father, Anton, Stefan's bride, Barbra, and Barbra's Tanta Gerta.

Gone now was the excitement of tourists of different nationalities coming into the shop; gone was the laughter and love which filled their lives. Stefan's father died, Tanta Gerta returned to Germany to care for Barbra's papa and now Barbra had gone to Germany.

Only Stefan, Ignatz, and the dog Pas now lived in the beautiful lonely building.

Studying Stefan, Ignatz asked, "Do you want something else? Instead of bread I can get some cheese or go out and buy some strudel."

Anton slammed his fist on the table in frustration. "What the hell am I going to do?" He looked at the startled Ignatz, "I haven't heard from Barbra for a month! Do I just sit here, doing nothing?"

Ignatz, always dressed in dark trousers, white shirt, slender ribbon tie, and apron, had been wondering the same about his own future. What was going to happen to him when Stefan and Barbra left for America? The Cunard ship passage for Barbra and Stefan was paid for through the local Zagreb bank. Ignatz had been sent to collect the boarding tickets for the Carpathia scheduled to leave Rijeka in a few days.

Ships could also be boarded in Trieste, but Stefan's hurt, combined with his annoyance towards Barbra prevented him from going to see his family there. He didn't want to explain that Barbra was not with him. Teta Sofie, who had spoiled Stefan as a child, was now with her husband, Alexie, the owner of the Renaldi Trading Company, living with their small son, Aleksy, on a hilltop villa overlooking the Adriatic.

The Croatian mountain dog, Pas, lying near the table, stood. With his ears up and tail wagging, walked towards the back entrance, before Ignatz or Stefan heard any movement.

Disappointed that it was only Dr. Josef Popovich and not Barbra, Stefan called out, "Come, have some coffee with me. We have some fresh bread."

Patting Pas' head as he walked alongside the dog, Dr. Popovich looked with disappointment at the dimly lit store of stacked boxes and crates.

"So, you are going?" said the doctor, slipping into a chair opposite Stefan. "Have you heard from Barbra?"

Ignatz brought a cup and poured coffee for the doctor.

Dr. Popovich had been the tall and very handsome physician who attended the ill Teta Sofie, before she realized she was pregnant. Later, after becoming friends with Barbra and Stefan, Dr. Popovich cared for Barbra when she became pregnant.

Stefan sipped his now cooled coffee and motioned for Ignatz to warm it.

"Barbra has not been the wife I had hoped for." complained Stefan. "She left me not knowing what prices to put on items and certainly she knew I could not make good offers on the items brought in for sale." There was anger and bitterness in his voice. "I had to close the store. Customers asked for her and when I told them I would help them, they excused themselves and said they would be back later."

As Ignatz warmed the coffee, Stefan lifted his cup saying, "Put some brandy in this."

On a side table were bottles of wine, slivovitz, kruskovac and some brandies. Dr. Popovich declined with a shake of his head when Ignatz offered him the brandy.

Stefan looked at the neatly-dressed doctor, wearing a grey wool suit and matching tie. Looking over his cup as he sipped the warm liquid Stefan said, "She wasn't much of a wife these past months." He put down his cup. "Barbra started sleeping alone. Lately I had to find affection elsewhere." The look of surprise on the doctor's face along with annoyance reflecting in his dark eyes, was unexpected by Stefan.

Before Stefan could say anything, Dr. Popovich set his coffee cup on the table, trying to control the anger in his voice said "She has lost two babies within thirteen months. She was terribly depressed and I am sure she was afraid of getting pregnant again." The doctor caught his breath and went on, "Barbra told me how disappointed you were when the boy babies died and she told me how you blamed her for being so weak."

The look of anger was evident on Stefan's face. His voice was controlled when he said, "How dare you discuss such personal and private matters with my wife."

"She was my patient." said the doctor. "I needed to know why she was so depressed. Not only was she saddened by the loss of the babies, but she was worried for her father."

Stefan rose from the table and stood facing the still seated doctor. "I should come first, not her father. I was so tired of hearing about Papa."

With a steady gaze, Dr. Popovich asked, "Why didn't you go with her to Germany? How could you let her go alone?" His voice was full of concern. "Ignatz could have stayed and watched over your closed store while you went with her."

Stefan stared in silence at Dr. Popovich who calmly returned the stare.

Ignatz stood away from the table moving near the doorway leading to his kitchen living area. He was heartsick. Stefan had become a stranger to him. The way he had been behaving and the way he spoke to his very good friend, the doctor, worried the servant greatly.

Josef Popovich stood, the palms of his hands resting on the table, ignoring the fly buzzing near his face. He looked at Stefan, saying, "A man does not turn his back on his wife when she is ill and depressed. I knew of her unhappiness and you disappoint me as a husband and a man."

Stefan turned his back on the doctor and started up the stairs leading to the living quarters above. He kept walking up as he said, "My affairs and those of my wife are none of your business."

The doctor stood waiting for Stefan to say something more, when Stefan disappeared up the stairs the doctor nodded goodbye to Ignatz, leaving through the back door.

From the upper landing, Stefan called down to Ignatz. "Get your things together. Call someone to transport these boxes to Rijeka. We are going to America, to a place called Gary to be with my cousin Katya."

For a moment, Ignatz was speechless. When he found his voice he called up to Stefan, “I am going with you? What about Barbra?”

“You are going with me,” called down Stefan, his hands resting on the ornate balcony railing. “Barbra chose her father over me.”

CHAPTER 2

Selo Strašnik, near Zagreb

In the village of Strašnik, near the Glina River, lived Ivanka Babich with her father and brother. Ivanka was a strong 16-year-old girl, thin, slender faced with hazel eyes. From the time she was 12 years old, after the death of her mother, Ivanka became the woman of the house, cooking, gardening, and caring for her father and brother.

The simple, one level Babich house was made of hewn wood. A barn stood behind the house, and there was a garden alongside the house with a well of good water close by. The yard was nicely fenced with interlaced twigs, keeping the pigs confined, but the chickens and a couple ducks wandered about freely. Each morning, after milking their only cow, Ivanka lead the animal to a nearby enclosed pasture for a day of grazing.

Now, in the simple one room house with a pounded dirt floor and white washed walls decorated close to the ceiling with red-stenciled designs, Ivanka sat on her straw mattress bed with a heavy heart. Her bed was at the far end of the room near the clay stove, enough away from her father and brother's beds to provide a bit of privacy.

She undid her braids and slowly ran a hand-carved bone comb through her long brown hair. Ivanka, alone in the house, put down her comb and sobbed with tears pouring down her reddened cheeks.

She was in love with Stanko Perpich, who left for America six months ago, promising to send for her. Ivanka waited hopefully each day for a letter which never came.

She was close to panicking because her brother was getting married and would be bringing his bride to this house. There could be no room for two women in the small house.

That sunny morning, her father, a small man, his skin wrinkled and dark from years of working in the fields, announced to Ivanka, "I have chosen a husband for you. He is from the next village." When Ivanka started to protest, he raised his hand to silence her. "You are an embarrassment to me and your brother. You have spurned every eligible man in the village and everyone is laughing at you for waiting for Stanko to send you a ticket which will never come."

"It will come." argued Ivanka in tears. "He promised."

"You are not waiting any longer." said her father, firmly. "Cook a nice dinner and make yourself look better. Your future husband is coming this evening."

Later, it was as if the chickens knew one of them was meant to be eaten. Ivanka chased them until she finally caught one. Not the plumpest one, but she really didn't care if she pleased her father, her brother, and the widower with two small children from Petrinja. After she stood with one foot on the chicken's wings and the other foot on the feet of the sacrificial bird, Ivanka slit its throat. When the chicken finished thrashing, she plucked its feathers, storing them in a large pillow case. Later the feathers would make up a pillow or a comforter.

She washed her hair in the cold well water, not taking the time to heat the water, making her head ache. Ivanka didn't wash her hair to look good for the widower, for she had other plans. Secret plans.

Ivanka's brother and father, both about the same height and build, with matching brown hair and eyes, washed at the well where Ivanka had laid out towels for them.

Ivanka's brother, Vujo, was a younger version of his father, also tanned from the sun, but not yet wrinkled.

The house was neat, baskets and buckets stored discreetly out of sight. The smells of cooking meat and baking bread whet the appetite. Both men were pleased with the table setting. A hand-embroidered cloth of red flowers and green leaves trailed along the edge of the material. A cup of wild flowers was on the center of the table and the red napkins on the table pleased her brother.

Vujo, delighted, whispered to his father, "I think she has decided to go along with the marriage."

Gossip in villages always travels quickly. For the villagers, gossip is not only a form of information, but entertainment.

Conveniently, all of Ivanka's curious neighbors found some task to keep them in front of their houses, close to the road, to see Ivanka's prospective husband.

In a farm wagon, pulled by a tired-looking black and grey horse, forty-year-old Nikola Todorich, extremely plain in looks and already balding, had his bridal gift in the back of the wagon.

Ivanka, dressed in a clean, long-sleeved blouse and skirt of homespun fabric, was humiliated as she had never been before. One's worth was determined by the proposal gift. To the amusement of her neighbors, instead of a handsome pig, cow, or bull, were two scrawny goats.

Ivanka smiled and bowed slightly upon meeting Nikola. He looked Ivanka over, as if he were purchasing livestock and smiled at her. It was then that Ivanka noticed Nikola had a front tooth missing.

The three men sat at the table eating, while Ivanka served them. Throughout the meal, Ivanka's father and brother praised her talents as a cook and hard worker. It was as though they were offering her for sale. Nikola grinned at his prospective bride, the missing tooth more evident than ever. Ivanka smiled sweetly in return.

Finished with the meal, her father and brother went outside, leaving Ivanka alone with Nikola. The man was shy, clumsy, and not sure how to court Ivanka. They sat side by side on the bench at the table. He reached for her hand, which she pulled away. She did the same when he tried to embrace her and she most certainly did not let him kiss her. His breath smelled of slivovitz, probably consumed before coming to Strašnik. Also, the smell of garlic seemed be coming from his pores. Disappointed, Nikola went outdoors to join the two men.

Nikola complained that Ivanka was not receptive to his advances. "I don't think she likes me," he complained. "Maybe I should take the goats and go home." Her annoyed brother hurried into the house, where Ivanka was clearing the dishes.

"What is wrong with you?" he demanded. "Couldn't you be nice to him? He thinks you don't like him." When Ivanka made no reply, Vujo said, "We are going to the gostiona…tavern, in Nikola's wagon. I don't know how long we will be." As an afterthought he said, "Drink some slivovitz, it might put you in a better mood for when we return. When we come back, and I don't care how late it will be, you go sit outside with him and let him know you are ready to get married."

In the yard, Ivanka saw the men off and smiled brightly as she waived goodbye. Back in the house, she left the dishes and did not put away the remaining food. Instead, she went to her bed where under it a cardboard suitcase was stored.

For six months Ivanka watched the mail for her ticket to America. She wasn't waiting any longer to hear from Stanko and she positively was not marrying Nikola. In the months while waiting, she sold eggs, cheese, whatever she could hide from her father and brother, secretly saving the money. She already had some clothes packed in the hidden suitcase. Around her waist she tied a belt from which hung an envelope-shaped cloth purse. Here she put her money, feeling it was safe close to her body. She wrapped a crocheted shawl around her shoulders, carried her wool coat in one hand and her suitcase in the other.

She didn't know where Gary, Indiana was, but remembered that Stanko told her he would find work there in the mills. She was determined to find Gary and her beloved Stanko. For six months she relived her last night with him, where hidden, they had made love in the forest. He promised…yes, he promised! "I will send you a ticket to come to America."

CHAPTER 3

Ivanka stayed off the roads as long as possible, fearing someone would recognize her. When she finally felt she was far enough from Strašnik, she left the woods and walked on the road. A few times a wagon would stop offering her a ride, but she refused. Ivanka was not comfortable with strangers, yet she was fearful of walking in the coming dusk.

When a horse drawn wagon full of people moved alongside her, it slowed. "How far you going?" asked the driver. Seeing so many people in the wagon, Ivanka wasn't so cautious. "I want to go to Zagreb." The man bent over, offering a rough calloused hand to Ivanka. "That is where we are going. Come on, you look tired."

He took her suitcase and coat, handing them back into the wagon as he pulled Ivanka up.

"Hvala…thank you." said Ivanka. She had never been this far from home. She moved back into the wagon where there were several women with children of assorted ages. All were dressed in their peasant skirts and shawls. It appeared they were also traveling a distance, for the wagon was loaded with cloth bundles and wicker suitcases tied with rope.

A woman older than Ivanka, with a young child dozing in her arms asked, "Do you have people in Zagreb?"

"No," said Ivanka, "I want to go to America."

"That is where we are going." said a young man, perhaps fifteen or sixteen years old, wearing faded brown pants and a collarless homespun shirt with long sleeves, buttoned at the wrist. "This is my mother sitting next to you and my baby sister." Ivanka smiled at the sad looking woman and nodded a greeting. The young man said, "Our Tata…father sent us tickets. We are supposed to meet other people in Zagreb and I think we are all going on the same ship."

Ivanka's heart quickened. These people were going to America!

She asked, "Do you know the people you are to meet?"

"No, but we were told that once we got to the square in Zagreb, someone from the ticket company would meet all the travelers and get them to the ship." The young man reached out his hand, "My name is Andra."

Ivanka took his hand and smiled at his mother, who looked worried and tired. Andra's mother was not only worried, but frightened. They were leaving their home with only what they could carry to go to a land they knew nothing about. Not good at making conversation with strangers, the jostling of the wagon and the fading of the day made Ivanka drowsy and she nodded off.

A thrilled Andra, his young face flush with excitement, gently shook Ivanka's shoulder. "We are here!" He shook her again. "Look, we are in Zagreb. Isn't it beautiful?"

The wagon wasn't moving. It was in a line of wagons all slowly entering the huge square in Zagreb. There were crowds of people already off the wagons, all with suitcases or bundles waiting to head for America. The expressions on their faces ran the gamut of excited, worried, and some just frightened. Someone helped Ivanka from the wagon, while Andra handed down her suitcase. She stood there, looking around at the confusion of excited people, unsure what to do.

It was only dusk with the sun glowing shades of red as it began its descent. As more people climbed down from the wagon, Ivanka felt herself being pushed out of the way and desperately hung onto her suitcase. She looked out at the buildings bordering the square. She saw beautiful, bright-colored stone buildings glistening in the sunlight. At the far end, she saw a tiled roof of many colors. She did not know this was Sveti Marko Crkva…St. Mark's Church, or that it had been built in the 13th century. On the roof was the Zagreb Coat of Arms made up of colored tiles.

Ivanka could smell food, making her aware she was hungry. She started to walk towards a table, but Andra pulled her away saying, "We have to follow the man holding the sign."

In the center of the crowd of travelers stood a man holding a huge, roughly drawn picture of a ship. He called out loudly, "Aide, pozuriti…come, hurry up. Get in line and show me your tickets."

Andra pushed Ivanka in line, behind his mother and sister. The young man had taken it upon himself to care not only for his mother, but also Ivanka.

When it was Ivanka's turn to show her ticket, she had none. "What are you doing here?" growled the annoyed man in charge. Before she could reply, Andra said, "She lost her ticket. She will pay you for another one." Ivanka, nervous, stood before the man. He was dressed in a dark blue suit, a yellow cravat, and on his head he wore a brown derby hat. He looked her over. "Is it true you lost your ticket?" When she nodded, he asked, "Where are you going in America?"

Without hesitation, she said, Gary, Indiana.

"Give me 75 krone."

Ivanka's mouth dropped. She didn't have that much money. "I don't have that much."

Annoyed at the line being help up, the agent said, "Sorry, step out of line."

Andra pushed his way in front of Ivanka and said to the agent, "She has already paid for the lost ticket. Can't you help her out? Where will she go, if not with us?" There were murmurs of agreement from the other passengers waiting to board the train.

"Give me what you have." growled the annoyed man, taking what paper money Ivanka handed him.

With her ticket safe in the purse attached to her belt, Ivanka felt as if she were in a daze. Confused and hungry, she allowed herself to be herded onto a train, staying close to Andra and his mother. She was frightened by the jostling of people pushing to board the train. Andra, anxious to find seats, pulled her by the hand fearing she would get lost in the crush of people. Boarding the train, Ivanka felt light-headed. There were so many people scrambling for seats, pushing, shoving.

Andra pushed his mother and little sister on the nearest seat, nearly flinging Ivanka on the seat opposite his mother, before someone else could occupy it. He seated himself next to her, pleased that the four of them had this small traveling space to themselves.

The noise and confusion made Ivanka's head reel. The bedlam of people pouring through the narrow aisles, the noise of the train whistle, and a man arguing with the conductor that he wanted to bring his two chickens with him added to the chaos. When the chickens were taken away from the man, his yelling and swearing brought loud remarks from the fellow passengers.

Night was fast approaching. Most of these people had never been on a train before. When it jerked and started to move, there were sounds of concern, along with "Sveta Majka…Holy Mother."

The slow, 160-kilometer ride from Zagreb to Rijeka was not very comfortable, still many of the exhausted riders dozed. Each car had one washroom, always with a line of people waiting to use it. Walking through the aisles was tedious because suitcases and other possessions were sometimes deposited there to make more room for seating.

Andra's mother shared their simple food with Ivanka. Ivanka was embarrassed to take the food, eating only a little of what was offered, which was bread and some hard cheese. In her hurry to leave Strašnik, Ivanka had not thought to bring food.

For some unknown reason, the train stopped several times during the night, causing concern with the fearful passengers. The trip from Zagreb to Rijeka should not have taken as long as it did. Daylight was breaking as the people disembarked the train, where a man dressed in the same type of suit and hat as the one taking tickets in Zagreb herded everyone off the train and into a group. They were not far from the docks. The smell of the Adriatic, the noisy gulls swirling overhead, the shouts of the dock workers, sounds of the ship whistles, and again the jostling of bodies, alarmed Ivanka. This time, she deliberately reached for Andra's hand and held it tightly.

It seemed as if Ivanka and her fellow passengers stood on the dock a very long time, waiting for the first- and second-class passengers to board. The third-class ticket holders were ushered to another gangway, this time not climbing upward, but walking almost straight onto the boat. Ivanka held on to the side rails, fearing she might fall into the water.

Once onto the *Laconia*, the third-class passengers were instructed to descend a staircase and find a cabin on their own. Again, Andra took charge, pulling and shoving Ivanka, his mother, and sister until they found a cabin, which was more dormitory style than a private cabin. "Sit on the bed and don't leave. Someone might take your spot." ordered Andra. He had talked with men who had returned from America, so he had an idea what to expect while on board the ship.

Exhausted Ivanka slept soundly that night. They all slept in the clothes they wore when leaving their homes. Ivanka wished she could bathe. There was a bucket of water outside their cabin door to use for washing.

The next morning, Ivanka pinned a cloth with her name written on it to her pillow, in the hopes her bed would still be hers when she returned from the deck. She desperately needed fresh air.

In the bright sunlight, Ivanka saw no chairs or benches for seating. It appeared that one could hardly find a place to sit for the number of people sprawled out on the deck.

Seeing an empty spot near some crates, Ivanka sat on the deck, placing her suitcase under her legs. The case was always with her, it held all she owned and she was fearful someone might steal it.

Her mind was a jumble of thoughts. What if she didn't find Stanko? Perhaps he was ill or something bad may have happened to him. What would she do? She couldn't return to her home. She looked at all the people enjoying the fresh air. With the gentle rocking of the ship, the sound of string instruments being played, and the warm sun on her body, it wasn't long before Ivanka closed her eyes. She awoke to the smell of cigarette smoke and the feel of a hand under her blouse. Ivanka didn't take the time to look at the man touching her. She jumped to her feet, grabbed her suitcase and used it as a weapon, striking the startled man in the head with it. There were other men nearby, laughing at Ivanka's attack. For the rest of the trip, Ivanka never went on deck without Andra or his mother at her side.

Ivanka's other fear was becoming infested with lice. She noticed some men on the deck scratching, pulling up their shirt sleeves and looking for crawling, biting insects. It was not unusual to see men remove their shirts and have a friend inspect their backs for lice. Ivanka was careful not sit near people she saw scratching.

During the 18-day crossing, there were two days of rough seas. Seasickness kept most of the passengers in their bunks. The steerage section smelled of vomit, the odor making persons even more ill.

With the rough seas, persons were allowed on deck, with instructions to hold on to the guide ropes while walking about.

Andra warned Ivanka, "Don't go out. Even with the ropes to hold, it is dangerous."

The ship *Laconia* was part of the English Cunard line. Several of the ship's crewmen were Croatians from Rijeka. It was pleasant to talk with them, to be able to ask questions without being treated as if one were stupid for not speaking English. Occasionally, one of the Croatian crew would bring fruit to Ivanka. She learned to peel a banana instead of trying to eat it with the skin. Once, when she bit into an apple and a worm wiggled in the bite spot, those around her laughed and said, "So you get a little meat with your fruit."

There was excitement and shouting from those on deck, when New York was in sight.

Once the ship was docked, Ivanka, among the other immigrants, was herded off the ship and onto benches in sectioned-off areas awaiting clearance. At Riker's Island, Andra once again took charge, keeping his tight group together. He knew no English, but watched the others in line before him, always careful not to say or do anything to bring suspicion to them. Each of them had to show the papers provided by the man who issued the boarding passes. Their names were confirmed, and sometimes misspelled. Andra became Andrew without him knowing it.

Each immigrant was seen by a doctor. Their lungs were listened to, and their tongues inspected. If any person had a persistent cough or a suspicious rash, they could be and often were returned to the country they came from.

The last task the travel agents had to perform was to put the people on the proper trains, depending on their destinations.

When the New York Central stopped in Pennsylvania, Ivanka felt panic. Andra had taken care of her and she felt confident and safe with him. It never occurred to her that they would be parting and that she would need to go on alone. Andra, his sister, and mother were going to meet his father in Pittsburgh. A very worried Ivanka would have to continue on alone to Chicago and then take another train to Gary.

When she had to say goodbye to her protector and his family, Ivanka was shaking and sick to her stomach. Andra gave Ivanka the thirty cents she would need for the train fare from Chicago to Gary.

Now, without Andra on the train, she sat curled in her seat next to the window, hoping no one noticed she was crying. Ivanka had no idea that going to America alone could be so uncertain and terrifying. She knew no English, and couldn't buy food or something to drink.

Oh, Dear God, how will I ever find Gary, Indiana and Stanko?

Ivanka felt someone sit next to her. She did not look up.

"Gospodicna…Miss, I heard you are going to Gary. I am going there also." His voice was gentle and kind and he spoke to her in Croatian. "My brother lives in Gary and he sent me my ticket. He told me what train to take how to contact him when I get to Gary."

Ivanka wiped her eyes with the corner of her shawl before turning to face the man. He was young and pleasant looking with a clear complexion, dark hair, and blue eyes. He was dressed wearing a nice pair of grey trousers with a darker grey jacket, much better than most of the men she had seen on the train or ship.

When Ivanka turned to face him, her eyes were red from crying. He introduced himself, "My name is Marjan Mandich."

Ivanka gave him a weak smile and said, "I am Ivanka Babich."

"Do you have family in Gary?" Marjan asked.

"No, I am coming to find my fiancé. I haven't heard from him for a while, I hope he is alright."

"When we get to Gary, my brother told me to call him on the telephone. He will come for me." explained Marjan. "I am sure he will help you, if he can."

Ivanka only nodded numbly, not knowing what a telephone was. Exhausted from fear and worry, she didn't feel like having conversation, so she looked out the window at the countryside, not interested in the scenery.

The young man touched her arm to get her attention. Ivanka looked away from the window to see him holding a piece of butcher paper, on it were a piece of cheese and hard sausage.

She was so very hungry inhaling the aroma of the food. Her eyes went from the food to Marjan's face.

"Take it." he said. "I have already eaten what I want."

Ivanka gratefully took the offered food, smiling shyly at Marjan.

"Hvala," she thanked him. It embarrassed her to have him watch her eat. It wasn't long before the rocking of the train, and the hypnotic rhythm of the wheels made her fall asleep again, her head leaning against the window.

Marjan picked up Ivanka's shawl which had dropped to the floor. He draped it across her chest like a small blanket.

Her coat was on her lap and he spread it out over her knees for warmth.

Just as Andra had looked after Ivanka on the ship, now Marjan watched over her. They took the train from Chicago to Gary along with several other immigrants. For most of them, this was the last leg of their journey from Europe. The mood on the train was thick with a mixture of excitement and trepidation. Many of them would be reunited with family they had not seen for a very long time. Ivanka hoped Stanko was alright. Several times she was sure he did not write because something may have happened to him.

From the train station in Gary at Third and Broadway, an excited Marjan found a phone and called his brother Tomo. When Marjan finished the call, he said to Ivanka, "Tomo will be here soon. I told him you were looking for someone and he said he would take you to a place where everyone gathers and perhaps someone will know your Stanko."

In a very short time, Marjan's brother arrived in a nice covered horse-drawn buggy. Ivanka watched with pleasure as Tomo and Marjan hugged and kissed each other repeatedly.

The brothers, tears of joy in their eyes, settled Ivanka in the buggy then headed for Milan's Tavern. Tomo gave Ivanka a warm smile, saying, "Milan's is the gathering place for the Croatians. If Stanko is in Gary, someone at Milan's will surely know him."

Ivanka noticed that Tomo was very well dressed in a three-piece suit of dark gabardine. A handsome chained pocket watch was visible on his vest. Tomo had lighter hair than his brother and wore a fashionable mustache. He was partners with Stevo Markovich in a fine furniture store which also provided funeral services.

Awed by the sights, Ivanka stared at the buildings lining Broadway. There were streetcars on rails, like trains. She couldn't imagine herself living in such a place. Where were the cows and chickens, she wondered.

As they continued to Milan's, the streets and houses became less impressive. Many resembled shacks. Now and then, someone along the street would call out to Tomo, giving him a wave of the hand. It was as if everyone knew him and that impressed his excited brother, who couldn't take in the sights fast enough.

Milan's Tavern was a wooden, rectangular building, unpainted, except for the large painted sign reading MILAN'S.

When the trio entered the friendly tavern, there were shouts of greetings from many people. Ivanka was self-conscious, aware that she had only changed her blouse and skirt once during the long trip. She was pleased that she had combed and braided her hair on the train from Chicago. The room was crowded with men in soiled, sweaty clothing, many just off their shift at the mill. The wooden bar with stools was situated at the entrance of the room against the wall, facing the room of mismatched tables and chairs. A haze of cigarette smoke hung above the room, like a cloud.

Milan, the owner, was a large man, who knew Tomo from the young man's first days in Gary when he had escaped from his obligation as an indentured farm worker. Tomo often sang with the tamburashi …musicians, and became a favorite of the customers.

With a friendly smile, Milan asked, "Who have we here, a brother? He looks like you."

"Yes," beamed proud Tomo. "We are finally together." Turning to his brother he said, "Marjan, meet my good friend Milan."

When Marjan extended his hand for a shake, Milan instead gave him a hug, saying, "I know I will love you just as I love Tomo."

Men gathered around Marjan, slapping him on the back, shaking his hand, someone handed him a drink, while others raised their glasses to toast him.

Milan's eyes moved to Ivanka, noticing she was an unmarried girl with her head uncovered and braids down her back. She stared in wonder at all the activity and warmth being showered on Tomo's bratso…brother.

"Are you a sister?" Milan asked, extending his hand.

Overcome with all the excitement and the men at the bar staring at her, she was too shy to reply. Tomo said, "She is looking for Stanko Perpich. Do you know him?"

"He is here." shouted Milan, taking a bewildered Ivanka by the arm, nearly dragging her to a table in the center of the room, where two men and two women were seated.

Hearing his name, a good looking, dark-haired man in his early twenties stood up and looked toward the sound of Milan's voice.

"Here I am. What…" Stanko, his dark eyes stared in disbelief. *It couldn't be! What was Ivanka doing here?*

Ivanka ran to Stanko. Before she could wrap her arms around him, he pushed her arms away. His words were barely a whisper, "Anka, what are you doing here?" Still smiling, a very happy Ivanka looked at her beloved. He was as she remembered him, a bit thinner, the beginning of a mustache, but still as handsome as she remembered him.

A short, very pregnant woman, with her hair covered in the custom of married Croatian women, stood and took Stanko's hand, asking "Muz…husband, who is this woman?" The slap Ivanka delivered to Stanko's face was so loud it nearly stopped all the conversation in the tavern. Stanko's pregnant wife moved past her shocked husband towards the red faced Ivanka.

Ivanka's hand was up in the air, ready to deliver a slap to Stanko's wife, when Milan with the grace of dancer, grabbed her hand, twirled her away from the table, past the bar towards his living quarters.

CHAPTER 4

The next morning was a Sunday. Stevo Markovich, owner of Markovich Furniture Store, read the various newspapers saved for him by the train conductors. For years he paid them for all the newspapers and magazines left by passengers.

An outdoor sitting area was new to the yard behind the building. Stevo, or Steve, as he was known by most of the non-immigrants, realized that the kitchen separated by only a door could still allow some of the cigarette odor to drift into the store.

Stevo, scanning the various newspaper headlines, did not hear the gate open. He jumped when a hand mussed his hair.

Stevo spun around to see his friend Milan grinning at him. Friends for years, always teasing or jabbing one another with friendly insults, Stevo said to Milan, "With all your sins, you should be in church."

With a hand he smoothed his hair, fixing his blue eyes on Milan, saying, "Sit down. Have some coffee with me." Stevo, always looking well put together, wore dark trousers, a white shirt with the sleeves rolled up without a tie. Already having shaved, his mustache was neat.

Milan pulled out the only other chair and sat down. He looked out into the large yard where a horse barn stood and another stored the various carriages or buggies needed for funerals. The Markovich Furniture Store also provided caskets and burial services.

Stevo called out towards the open kitchen door, "Ignatz, another cup and some coffee."

Surprised, Milan asked, "Where is Cleona?"

Cleona was the black woman who had been his cook and later, the business partner of Stevo's wife Katya. The two women started a successful lotion and cream business called Royal.

Before Stevo could reply, Ignatz was there with a tray. He nodded at Milan saying, "Dobro jutro...Good morning." He served the coffee in his usual manner of pouring warm milk and coffee simultaneously into the cup. "Here are some kiflice...nut horn cookies, to go with the coffee."

"Hvala...thank you." said a smiling Milan.

Ignatz made a slight bow, then headed for the barn where Bobo lived. The black man had worked for Stevo from the time the store opened, doing repairs, tending the horses, and often driving the carriages for funerals.

Again Milan asked, with his mouth full of a horn cookie, "Where is Cleona?"

Stevo sighed, and sipped his coffee before saying, "When she found out Ignatz could cook and run the kitchen, she asked to leave."

From the look on Milan's face, Stevo could tell Milan needed more information, so Stevo continued. "The salesman who was buying up the Royal products hasn't been coming around as often as he used to...since...since Katya has been gone."

The friends sipped their coffee in silence. At the mention of Katya and her death, both men couldn't speak, feeling the pain of her loss.

Feeling the silence becoming uncomfortable, Stevo said, "Cleona has hired some black women to help her prepare the creams and soaps. She also has women selling them door to door for her."

Seeing the surprised look on Milan's face, Stevo continued. "From what I hear she is doing well and making more money paying the women less than by selling wholesale to Jim Slade."

Ignatz appeared with more coffee, refilling the cups. He promptly disappeared into the kitchen.

Milan sipped his coffee while admiring the pots of brightly colored flowers bordering the patio. He said, "I met Tomo's brother last night. Are they still sleeping?"

"Oh, no, they left early for a tour of the city. Marijan was anxious to see everything." said Stevo.

Milan pulled a pack of Camels from his pocket. This was a new, packaged cigarette introduced by the Reynolds Tobacco Company that year. He offered the opened pack to Stevo, who took one saying, "I haven't tried these yet. Are they any good?"

"Better than the ones I roll for myself." said Milan, holding a lit match for Stevo.

The friends smoked without speaking, the silence broken by the whinny of a horse as a wagon rolled on the unpaved street in front of the store.

Stevo said, with a mischievous glint in his eyes, "So…where did the young girl who hit Perpich spend the night?"

"I see Tomo and Marijan told you about it." Milan blew cigarette smoke away from the table. "I had to pull her away. She was going to hit Perpich's pregnant wife."

"You haven't answered my question," urged Stevo, "Where did she spend the night?"

Disgusted, Milan flicked his cigarette onto the soil in the yard. "In my bed! Is that what you wanted to hear?" His eyes narrowed as he said, "And I slept in the bar and not in the bed." Now he had a twinkle in his eye as he said, "I don't understand how you can think I would take advantage of a young girl."

"Oh, Sveti Isus…Holy Jesus," said Stevo sarcastically, "why would I think such a thing, especially since I know you so well?"

"Yeba te," swore Milan. "I came here for a reason."

"Oh?" said Stevo, crushing his finished Camel cigarette in his coffee saucer.

"I need some clothes for Ivanka. That's her name." said Milan. She has been living in two outfits for almost a month."

Stevo was taken aback by the request. His face registered painful sadness only briefly, but Milan saw it and understood.

Milan said, "I know, I know. It wasn't easy for me to ask for some of Katya's clothes, but Ivanka needs a couple more outfits."

Stevo rose quickly so Milan would not see the tears in his eyes. He said, "I'll be right back.

Milan left the table and wandered about the backyard of the store. He greeted Bobo, patted a couple horses on their rumps, then walked to the open gate and looked out onto street. He lit another cigarette and leaned against the gate. When he worked temporarily for Stevo, he would go out on the walkway to smoke. He wasn't aware the memory made him smile, for those were fun days, days when both he and Stevo tried to outwit one another for Katya's affection.

Returning, Stevo found Milan by the gate. He handed a pillowcase in which were two outfits. He said, "Give the pillowcase to Tomo the next time he is at your place."

"Why don't you come yourself?" said Milan. "I miss your sarcastic company."

"I don't like to be gone from the store. I feel I should be here since Katya's cousin Stefan is staying with me."

Milan frowned. "He came to my place once, he wasn't very friendly."

Not wanting to be overheard, Stevo took Milan by the arm. "Let me walk a ways with you."

"You don't trust him?" said Milan as they walked away from the gate.

"I expected him to help in the store, since he had one in Zagreb." Stevo shook his head, "He doesn't say anything, but I can feel he thinks my store does not have the quality of merchandise he expected."

Milan stopped walking and looked at his friend. "Did he say that?"

Stevo sighed trying to find a way to explain what he was feeling. Then said, "Stefan has the paintings and sculptures he brought from his store on display in my place. He lets me know the pieces have great value and mentions that I do not have the type of buyers who appreciate or can afford his things."

Stevo stopped walking. Scratching his chin, he said, "From what I gather, the Americans that visited his Zagreb store were not the type of people he finds here in our part of Gary. Most were wealthy world travelers, certainly not like our mill or factory workers."

Milan tucked the pillow case with the clothes under his arm and offered Stevo another cigarette. After blowing a plume of smoke into the air, Stevo said, "Hard to believe Stefan and Ivan were brothers." At this remark, Milan's jaw dropped. "Brothers?" He said in a surprised tone. "Brothers!" he said again, "That is hard to believe."

Stevo took another drag on his pre-rolled cigarette, "I have been remembering things that Katya told me. If I am remembering correctly, Stefan's father had an affair with Ivan's mother, meaning to marry her, but his father had already made marriage arrangements for him with a woman he considered a more suitable bride."

"I don't understand." said Milan. "Wasn't Ivan educated by this father?"

"Anton Vladeslav did not want to disobey his father, so he married his father's choice, Ernesta. He arranged for his pregnant lover to marry the local blacksmith, who raised Ivan. In order to stay close to Ivan, Anton Vladeslav saw to it that he became the boy's Godfather."

The two friends started to walk again, taking their time. Stevo said, "I understand that the Vladeslavs are great land owners. The land was awarded to some previous Vladeslav warrior for duty to some King, I don't recall."

"Sveti Isus…Holy Jesus," said Milan, "does this mean the Vladeslavs have a title?"

"I don't know," said Stevo. "From the way Stefan behaves, I feel he expects me to bow when he enters the room."

"Bullshit," said Milan, using an American term he liked. "I know we aren't all treated the same in America, but we are supposed to be." Stevo laughed, "Either you are reading books or you are sleeping with a school teacher."

"Go to hell!" laughed Milan, waving the pillow case in the air as he crossed the street heading to his tavern.

When Milan entered his tavern, there were only a few men at the bar and in a far corner of the room, two men were at a table having what looked to be a private conversation.

Furiously scrubbing the tables was Ivanka, bucket in one hand, scrub brush attacking the top of the table, while a cloth for drying was draped over her shoulder. Scrubbing was her way of taking out her anger towards Stanko for lying to her.

Milan grabbed Ivanka's hand to stop the scrubbing. He said, "Come, let's sit and talk."

Milan's tone when he said, "Let's sit and talk", worried Ivanka. She followed him to a nearby table and sat down. She wondered if he was going to send her away. Where would she go? She had no money and the only person she knew was Marjan from the train ride.

Milan put the pillow case holding the clothes on the table. He waived to his brother, Mato, to join them. Mato was smaller than Milan, with the same color brown hair, but much younger looking. He said, looking from Milan to Ivanka "Is something wrong?"

"Nothing is wrong." said Milan. "I was wondering when the house will be finished." Milan was referring to the house being built in back of the tavern, where fruit trees once stood and goats lived. Now the trees and goats were gone and a wooden two story structure was there.

"The outside is done, but we still need to finish off the inside. Inside doors need to be hung and walls finished." Mato looked back towards the bar, should a customer need something to drink. No one looked at him, so he said to Milan, "Why do you ask?" "I am not too happy sleeping on two tables pushed together." said Milan. "Do you think Ivanka could sleep in the house?"

"Sure, "said Mato, "there are locks on both outside doors. It would be safe."

Milan turned to Ivanka, "Would you be afraid to sleep in the house alone?"

Ivanka didn't reply. She wasn't listening to the conversation. Her mind was in a whirl. She was sure Milan wanted her to leave because she took his bed and he had slept in the bar.

Mato nudged her arm. "Ivanka," he said, "are you listening?" She felt his nudge, raising her eyes, she saw both men looking at her. Tears filled her eyes as she said, "Where can I go? Please don't make me leave. I will sleep on the floor behind the bar. I won't take your bed." The words rushed out of her.

Milan and Mato looked from Ivanka to one another bewildered. Milan said, "Didn't you hear anything we said?"

Ivanka could only shake her head. Her eyes were wet and her cheeks were pink.

Mato almost melted seeing Ivanka so worried. "Ivanka," he said, "we are building a house in back. It isn't finished, but you can sleep there at night." Then he quickly added, "No one will bother you there."

Ivanka looked from Mato to Milan. "I have no money." she said.

Milan was touched by this remark. She was a simple peasant and not his type, but he felt there was something really good about her. He said, "We aren't asking for any pay. You can clean our rooms and the tavern."

Her eyes were wide with wonder. It was as if she still didn't understand.

Mato said, "Come with me. I will show you the inside of the house."

Ivanka started to rise when Milan said, "Wait." He gave her the pillow case with the two outfits Stevo had chosen for her.

She opened the pillow case and looked inside. "Are these for me?" Her eyes were full of wonder as she felt the soft fabric. She pulled out a green peasant blouse. "These are beautiful."

Milan promptly said, "I know, I know. You don't have any money."

Mato immediately recognized it as having been worn by Katya. He smiled at his brother. He thought it nice of Milan to get them for Ivanka.

Men were coming in the door with a loud burst of conversation and laughter. The room was starting to fill with workers coming off their shift. Milan waived for Mato to take Ivanka to the house, while he went to the bar and greeted the men, “Kako ste?...How are you? Pivo…beer, rakiya…whiskey?

CHAPTER 5

The morning was warm with a gentle breeze and the aroma of nearby flowers scented the air. Stevo was still sitting at the table when Stefan came outdoors. Looking up he said, “Good morning.” Stefan was dressed in a cream-colored soft fabric shirt and dark trousers. Instead of a tie, he had an ascot at his neck. The ascot somewhat surprised Stevo, as the neckwear was not common in Gary.

As he sat down, Stefan only nodded to Stevo, not saying good morning. Ignatz appeared with coffee for Stefan and looked to Stevo to see if he wanted more. Stevo smiled covering his cup with his hand, indicating he didn’t want more. Stevo pushed some of the newspapers toward Stefan saying, “These are the papers delivered to me this morning. Perhaps you would like to look through them.”

As a youth, Stefan had been educated at University in Zagreb and both he and his half-brother, Ivan, spoke and understood the English language. Ignoring the offer, Stefan let out a sigh and asked in a somewhat condescending tone, “How is it you don’t have an automobile?” Stevo was taken aback by the question. First, Stevo didn’t care for Stefan’s manner of asking and second, Stevo almost found the question rude, as it was none of Stefan’s business.

“I don’t need an automobile.” said Stevo, looking directly at Stefan and keeping his tone controlled. “I have several carriages, a wagon, and some horses to take me when I need them. And,” he added “there are street cars on Broadway which can take you to 5th Avenue in a matter of minutes.” Stefan looked out into the yard, instead of at Stevo.

“I don’t enjoy riding the streetcar with the mill workers.” he said.

"I am sorry." said Stevo. "You can ask Bobo if he is free to take you in one of the carriages."

Stefan rose, leaving his coffee untouched. "I would like to use the phone to make arrangements if you don't mind."

Stevo kept his expression calm and only nodded to the use of the phone, which was in the store. Stevo didn't like Stefan. If he had not been Katya's cousin, Stevo would have asked him to leave after the first few days. For a month, Stevo tolerated Stefan's superior attitude. Not once did Stefan show any gratitude for a place to sleep, food to eat, or a place to unload and display his trunks of merchandise.

During the first week of Stefan's arrival, Stevo asked Stefan if he would watch the store for a couple of hours, Stefan had left the room with the question unanswered.

Stevo noticed that as time passed, Ignatz appeared wary of Stefan. When they had first arrived, Ignatz seemed very comfortable with Stefan. But now, Ignatz barely spoke to his employer and spent most of his time with Stevo or visiting Bobo in the barn. Through the kitchen door, Stevo could see that Stefan was going upstairs to the living area.

"Sit down, Ignatz." said Stevo. "I want to talk with you."

Ignatz looked surprised and even a bit suspicious. This was the first time in the month of their arrival in Gary that he had been asked to sit with Stevo.

Seeing Ignatz's hesitation, Stevo said, "Please sit. Let's talk."

Nervously the little man wiped his hands on his black apron and sat on the chair Stefan had occupied earlier. He looked at Stevo showing concern. *What did this mean? Was Stevo displeased with him?*

"How long have you worked for Stefan?" Stevo asked, nodding for Ignatz to help himself to the coffee. The man was so nervous he declined the offer. "Probably five years."

Ignatz's throat was dry and he was very nervous. "How is it you have stayed with Stefan for such a long time? It appears he doesn't treat people nicely." said Stevo.

Ignatz looked at Stevo a long moment before replying. His face displayed an array of emotions, from worry to concern, then sadness. He heard a church bell somewhere in the distance, smelled the dust in the air from a passing wagon, heard a dog bark, and from the street a woman's laughter. When he spoke, his voice was soft. "Stefan wasn't always the man you see now." He paused wanting to find the right words. "You see, the first day I met Stefan and his father, I was living in the closed building he had inherited. I had no right to be in the building." Ignatz spread his hands flat on the table, as if pressing them down, would help him find the right words. "Stefan and his father were so very kind. They gave me money to buy food and later money for proper clothes, because they hired me to look after them while they stayed in the old gambling house."

"When did he change? What made him change?" asked Stevo, offering Ignatz a cigarette. The nervous man only shook his head indicating he didn't want one.

"It began about a year ago." Ignatz hesitated speaking for he felt he had no right to talk against his employer.

Stevo saw the hesitation, saying, "Go on Ignatz. You are no longer his servant."

When Stevo saw the wide-eyed look of surprise on the little man's face, he said, "You are really working for me."

Ignatz's jaw dropped. Stevo continued, "Don't you see that it is I who provide you with the loft above the kitchen where you sleep? It is my food you eat?" Stevo continued, "I am sure that Stefan has not paid you anything while you have been here." Before Ignatz could make a reply, an automobile horn sounded on the street outside the gate. Stevo went to see about the noise.

Before he made it out the gate, Stefan, dressed in a fine gray suit and matching Homburg hat, brushed passed Stevo going directly to Adele Manning's white Chalmers Touring Car.

What the hell? Thought Stevo, so this is why he was going to downtown Gary so often. Somehow Stefan had met Adele, the same wealthy Adele who purchased many pieces of furniture from Stevo for her elegant apartment in the wealthy section of Gary. The same Adele Stevo had occasionally dated before he married Katya.

As the touring car pulled away from the store, Tomo and Marjan, in the fancy horse drawn carriage, were returning through the open gate.

Both young men alighted, while Bobo came to take care of the horses and carriage.

"That was Adele Manning." said a surprised Tomo. "How did that get started?"

Stevo scratched his chin and shook his head in wonder. "I have no idea," he said, "but it explains why he is gone so much."

Ignatz rose from the table to make room for Marjan and Tomo. He was relieved for their arrival interrupted Stevo's questions. Questions he didn't want to answer.

"Are you hungry?" asked Ignatz.

"We left before having breakfast and it is almost noon now. Give us whatever you have." said Tomo, "No need to make a big meal."

A breeze picked up and blew dust and sand in the air.

"Let's go inside." said Stevo. "Or you will be eating sand with your food."

The kitchen was a long rectangular room with the entrance door in the center. At the far right, Tomo and Marjan shared what was once Stevo's room. At the far left was a stairway leading to the loft, where Ignatz now slept. The well equipped kitchen had an Acme Regal Steel cooking range which could use coal or wood. It had six cooking holes and a high closet warming reservoir.

Ignatz loved this stove. He set about building a fire so he could make Palachinke…cheese crepes. He was left a bit uncomfortable with Stevo's questions about Stefan.

As Marjan was not speaking English yet, the conversation was in comfortable Croatian. The stirring wind outdoors was ignored as the kitchen filled with the delicious aroma of sweet cheese crepes.

"So where have you two been all morning?" asked Stevo, lighting up another cigarette.

"We have been to Milan's." said Marjan.

His brother laughed saying, "In hopes of seeing Ivanka." Tomo poured a sweet watered down wine in each glass, which was sometimes served with daytime meals.

"So," asked Stevo, "how is Ivanka doing?"

Ignatz carried three plates at one time, placing the first before Stevo.

A disappointed Marjan said, "She wasn't there." Seeing the questioning look on Stevo's face, he said, "And I didn't ask where she was."

Stevo patted Marjan on the shoulder saying, "She will be there the next time you go."

The phone, which was in the store, rang as the three were finishing their second serving of palachinke.

Tomo hurried through the kitchen door to the phone. "Stevo, it is for you. It is John, the manager from the Gary Hotel."

Stevo took the receiver from Tomo's hand, "Yes, John. I am here. What do you need?"

The voice on the phone said, "Steve, there are a man and a woman sitting in our lobby with trunks and cases asking for you."

For a moment Stevo was speechless. He asked "Did they say who they were?"

"Dr. Popovich and Madam Vladeslav." said John.

For a long moment, Stevo didn't reply. His mind was a jumble of thoughts. Who were this doctor and Madam Vladeslav? How did they come to call him?

Stevo said, "I will be down with a carriage as soon as I can."

"Better bring a larger carriage, there are trunks and baggage." said John.

To Tomo, Stefan said, "Have Bobo, get the larger carriage ready. I have to pick up a couple of people at the hotel. Make sure the cover is latched. It is windy out there."

Stevo turned to Ignatz, "Do you know Dr. Popovich and a Madam Vladeslav?"

Ignatz's eyes widened and his jaw dropped. He was so surprised that for a moment he could not speak. Finally he said, "Madam is Barbra Vladeslav, Stefan's wife. Dr. Popovich has been a good friend of both Stefan and Barbra. He was also Barbra's doctor."

A bit annoyed, Stevo said, "Stefan didn't bother to tell me I was having more guests."

"I don't think Stefan knew." said Ignatz. "I believe he didn't expect to see Barbra again."

Tomo and Marjan stood outside the kitchen door, feeling the sand stinging their faces. "Do you want us to go with you?" asked Tomo.

"Bobo and I will go." said Stevo. "You stay to answer the phone." To Ignatz, he said, "Just in case the doctor is also staying with us, you and Marjan can take a small bed from the store and put it in the sitting room. Prepare it with the bedding and pillows. No one uses that room anymore."

When Stevo and Bobo arrived at the entrance to the Gary Hotel, John the manager was waiting outside for them. "In here, Steve." He said. "You may want to hurry before the storm hits."

The lobby of the Gary Hotel had large, tall windows, from which gray and maroon velvet panels hung. The carpet had an oriental design in colors of gray, maroon and orange. The comfortable overstuffed chairs were a darker gray, complimenting the décor of the room.

Stevo spotted the trunks and luggage stacked near the door. John took Stevo by the arm and led him to an ornate gilded three-legged table with a white marble top. Stevo only saw the back of the woman, wearing a traveling suit with a brown, slim ankle-length skirt topped with brown jacket. Her wide brimmed hat sported an ostrich plume.

The man with her, Dr. Popovich, was facing the door and saw John leading Stevo to the table. He rose and walked towards Stevo. Smiling, he extended his hand, "Mr. Markovich, thank you so very much for coming."

It was then that Barbra turned and looked at Stevo, who had to catch his breath. She was beautiful and she had red hair! Katya's hair had been red.

Bobo, with the help of a porter, was hauling the trunks and suitcases to the carriage.

Stevo shook Dr. Popovich's extended hand then turned to Barbra Vladeslav, who rewarded him with a beautiful smile.

"Thank you, Mr. Markovich. We had found your address at our store in a letter from Katya." She saw the surprised look on Stevo's face. "Is something wrong?" she asked.

Stevo said, "My wife, Katya, died almost a year ago. My letter to you must have gotten lost."

A concerned hotel manager said, "Steve, the wind is picking up. You really should hurry."

"Thanks John. I appreciate the call." Stevo patted John's chest, at the same time dropping a folded bill in the breast pocket of the blond man's suit.

Barbra straightened up gathering up her beaded purse and her dark brown velvet stole.

At the sound of a familiar voice she turned to face a startled Stefan. He went pale at the sight of her.

Barbra said nothing. With her face expressionless, she turned, continuing out the door and let Josef Popovich help her into the carriage.

Alongside Stefan, blond Adele Manning, looking magnificent in a pale lilac day dress said, "Hello Steve. I haven't seen you in a long time."

CHAPTER 6

It was summer, yet the pelting rain was cold. There was no conversation on the short ride from Fifth Avenue to 14th Avenue where Stevo's store was located.

Josef Popovich tried once or twice to break the strained silence by thanking Stevo again for coming for them and asking how far they had to travel to the store. Barbra said nothing. Stevo and Bobo were in the front seat of the carriage, while Barbra and Josef occupied the second seat. When Stevo glanced back at Barbra, her face was expressionless, showing no anger, hurt and no tears. Josef stole side glances at Barbra, watching for any emotional signs, but he saw none.

Reaching their destination, Bobo stopped the carriage as close to the kitchen entrance as possible, so that his passengers could get into the building without getting soaked. Ignatz was waiting with a kišobran…umbrella, holding it open ready to assist. His face broke into a happy smile when he saw Barbra and took her hand to help her step off the carriage. The wind whipped the hard rain from a downward angle to a stinging sideways pelting.

Tomo and Marjan were waiting at the kitchen entrance. Barbra Vladeslav was a pleasant surprise to the young men. She was beautiful. Marjan pulled out a chair at the table for Barbra. Josef was right behind her and a chair was waiting for him.

Barbra and Josef glanced around the kitchen and up at the men who tried not to stare at them. Tomo reached out his hand to Barbra, "I am Tomo Mandich. I work with Stevo." Reaching for his brother's elbow and gently pushing him forward, he said, "This is my brother, Marjan. He just arrived yesterday." Barbra smiled, nodded a greeting while deep inside of her soul she was sorry for making the journey to America.

Ignatz appeared with towels which he had warmed on the stove, to wrap around Barbra's shoulders. The towel he offered to Josef was rejected with a grateful smile and shake of the doctor's head. Marjan looked out the open doorway. He said, "It looks as if the rain is slowing. As soon as it has stopped, we will bring your luggage in."

Stevo sat at the table opposite the doctor. "I hope you won't be disappointed with the room we have for you." said Stevo. "You see we only needed a living space for Katya and me."

Before Josef could reply, Barbra said, "I am embarrassed that we have intruded on you this way." She paused, wanting to find the right words. "You see, I thought Stefan wanted me to join him." Remembering the beautiful woman with Stefan at the Gary Hotel, Barbra's voice failed her and she couldn't go on.

Now Stevo disliked Stefan even more for not acknowledging his wife when he saw her at the hotel.

Ignatz put cups and glasses on the table, for the warmed wine and the steaming chai…tea he had prepared. He poured the tea for Barbra, already knowing her preference. For the men it was the warm wine.

Tomo and Marjan, their faces bright with interest at the arrival of these interesting people, sat together on a bench near the table, watching and listening.

Josef noticed Barbra's hand trembled slightly when she picked up her tea cup. She saw the concerned look in his eyes and quickly used both hands to steady the cup.

The look the doctor gave Barbra did not go unnoticed by Stevo. He said, "Madam Vladeslav, if you would like to lie down, Ignatz can show to your room."

"Please call me Barbra." she said, removing her large hat and placing it on a nearby chair. Her hair, not dark red as Katya's had been, but a golden red, was fashioned on her head in the Gibson Girl style. She said, "I can see our arrival was unexpected and possibly inconvenient for you. Perhaps we could go to a hotel."

"Oh, no." said Tomo, who was more than a little fascinated by Madam Vladeslav. He looked to Stevo, "If you would prefer, Marjan and I could move into the barn with Bobo if it would help."

Stevo wanted to smile, but kept it from showing. "Not necessary." He said, "The accommodations aren't perfect, but for now they will work." Ignatz was at Barbra's side, taking her hand in his. "Come Barbra, I will show you to your room." Barbra smiled at everyone, picked up her hat and allowed Ignatz to show her the way upstairs to the room Stefan was using.

The sun was trying to peek out of the clouds and the rain was now only a drizzle. Marjan and Tomo went outside to bring in the trunks and valises. Josef started to follow the young men to help, but Stevo stopped him with a hand on the doctor's arm. "Let them take the luggage upstairs. I want to talk with you."

Ignatz was soon helping with the lugging and hauling of trunks up the stairs to the upper living area. As Stevo watched them taking the luggage upstairs, he realized having so many people going up and down the stairs during store hours might distract the customers. When it was just he and Katya, they were careful not to disrupt business, but with three others using the stairs, it could be a distraction.

Stevo offered Josef a cigarette saying, "Stefan has been here a month and I really know nothing about him. His manner is cool and condescending, which as his host, I find rude."

Stevo held a light for Josef's cigarette, saying "Stefan completely ignored his wife at the hotel. He behaved as though he did not know her." Then he added, "Barbra's composure is amazing."

"It won't last." said the doctor. "I have watched her ever since she lost the first baby." Josef looked out into the distance trying to find the right words. "You see, she has this fantastic strength." Then he added, "But, there comes a time, when she is alone, that the strength disappears and she comes close to falling apart. That is why I came with her to America. She had just buried her father and came to Zagreb to find her husband gone and their home and business boarded up." He sipped from his wine glass and blew a stream of cigarette smoke into the air. "I am waiting for her to let go…to fall apart." Seeing Stevo's concern he added, "Don't worry. I am never far from her. I know when to mix the calming powder in her water and get her to drink. The powder makes her sleep and when she wakes she is herself again. This only started when she lost the first baby."

Stevo said, "I think Ignatz said something about the babies."

Josef continued, "Stefan was almost mean in his attitude towards Barbra after the first baby died. Then after the second was stillborn, he was close to cruel. It was as if he thought she had deliberately deprived him of the babies." The doctor paused, waiting for a reaction from Stevo, seeing none, he continued. "Also, Stefan resented Barbra's knowledge and her business abilities. It was she who made the business of VLADESLAV COLECIJA the success it became. She tried to make him part of it by introducing him to buyers, but it wasn't long before the buyers realized it was Barbra who was the knowledgeable one." The doctor looked about to see that no one was nearby listening. "Stefan became so determined to have a Vladeslav heir that he became possessed with trying to impregnate Barbra, who was in fear of losing another baby. She would come to my office and cry until she made herself ill. It was then she no longer slept with Stefan. This enraged him."

Josef stopped speaking when Tomo and Majan entered the kitchen, done with depositing the luggage in the proper rooms.

Tomo was quite comfortable joining the men at the table, while Marjan was a bit reserved. After all, he didn't know how he would fit into the Markovich business and household. Stevo said to Tomo, "Pour yourselves some wine, while I show the doctor around." Seeing Stevo snuff out his cigarette, Josef did the same, before they walked through the door that was the entry into the store.

Josef was almost taken aback at the size of the rectangular room full of ornately carved furnishings along with some which were simpler. Josef saw no dust on the clean, shiny furniture. The outer wall had windows halfway down so the merchandise could be viewed from the street. The inner wall had a stairway leading up to the living area.

The doctor stopped and touched a porcelain figurine. "I remember this from the store in Zagreb. Has Stefan sold any of his things here?" Stevo shook his head saying, "No. Most of my customers are the mill workers and they aren't looking for decorative pieces, they want only necessary furnishings."

Stevo and Josef, very comfortable with each other, turned to walk back towards the kitchen. It was then the doctor noticed the velvet curtain hanging next to the desk at the back wall. Stevo saw the doctor's gaze and led him to the curtain, pulling the cord which drew the curtain aside, displaying the assorted coffins stored there.

A slightly surprised Josef said, "You also sell these?"

Stevo nodded, explaining, "When necessary we also help the family with all the burial arrangements." Josef looked at the assortment of burial boxes. He saw very plain wooden boxes, a tiny one for infants, one with a bell on the outside. The bell was for a buried person who may not have been dead and could pull a cord to alert someone to free them from the casket. The one that caught Josef's attention was the metal casket with an oval glass in the lid so that the body could be viewed. Josef said, "The only time I have seen such a casket was when a high Zagreb official died."

Stevo noticed it was nearing four in the afternoon. The rain had stopped and an already waning sun was trying to peek out of the clouds. Stevo said to Josef, "Let me show you to your room. Perhaps you would like to take a nap before supper."

Once upstairs, Josef noticed a long narrow hallway. Stevo pointed to a door on the right, "That is my room. Your room is the next doorway on the left." Stevo added, "I hope you won't be too disappointed in the room. When we had this level added, we planned it only for Katya and me...and possibly a child."

"Please," said the doctor, "I feel we are imposing. I appreciate your hospitality."

"Stefan and Barbra's room is the third door on the right." said Stevo. "Come down whenever you want. Someone is almost always in the kitchen."

Before descending the stairs, Stevo took a look down the hallway. He wanted to check on Barbra to see if she needed anything. Before he got to the door of her room, he saw the chapel door open. It was the chapel he had made as a surprise gift for his beloved Katya, because she spoke so often of the chapel at Vladezemla in Croatia.

Sitting on the church pew, which had been cut to fit the small chapel, was an expressionless Barbra.

CHAPTER 7

The following morning, in Adele Manning's beautiful rented house on the west side of Fifth Avenue in Gary, Stefan awoke before Adele. He was in the floral wallpapered breakfast room, on the second floor of the house, which overlooked the gardens below. Stefan liked it here. He believed he belonged in such opulent surroundings, instead of the upper level of the Markovich furniture store.

Stefan was thinking about his mother Ernesta and her unhappy marriage to Anton. Their marriage had been arranged by their parents. Ernesta was agreeable to the marriage, as she knew when Anton's father passed away, Anton would be the Count of Vladezemla. The title and land had been bestowed on a distant Vladeslav warrior by some Hungarian or Austrian king.

When Stefan's father became the new Count of Vladezemla, it meant nothing to him. He was more interested in sharing the land with the people who lived on it. His terms were very generous to those who worked their own pieces of land or for Anton's estate. If any invitations of a royal nature came to Anton, he never acknowledged them. Ernesta was never to live the life of a Countess. To her great unhappiness, she had been destined to live as a landowner's wife.

Stefan recently had been thinking about his travels with Magda, the brothel owner who left the building in Zagreb to him. They had traveled and lived like royalty, never claiming to be such, but their money, made from gambling, along with their expensive clothing and superb manners led all to believe them to be royalty.

At a dinner party given by Adele, where most of the guests were wealthy railroad or steel men, Stefan casually mentioned that in Europe he was a Count, which indeed upon the death of his father, he became. Adele could hardly believe her luck. She was in love with a real Count and it appeared that he loved her in return. It was of no importance to her that Stefan had very little money compared to her. His money would have been enough if he chose to live modestly, but he wanted what Adele and her friends had.

Because Adele was the widow of a wealthy steel mill investor, she knew most of the people in power. Not only those running the mill, but others such as Gary's Mayor Knotts and Judge Gary.

Wealthy Chicago businessmen often came to a hunting area near the intersection of 25th Avenue and Clark Road. The area of 5,000 fenced–off acres was known as the Tolleston Club. Poachers were often beaten and there had been some bloody battles there until in 1908, a state law was passed allowing hunting on uncultivated land. By the time Stefan came to Gary, this area became the Gary Country Club with a golf course.

The men Stefan met at the club invited him to hunt. He wasn't fond of hunting, but wanted to be included in the company of these successful men. Most of all, he enjoyed being invited to the card games following the hunt. He was a skilled card player and had learned much about card players from his travels with Magda. Adele saw to it that he had the proper clothes which were kept at her home.

Stefan never mentioned a wife. And…he wasn't going to.

It was a little after eight a.m. in the kitchen in the back of Stevo's store. Ignatz was already at the stove frying up slanina…bacon. The delicious smell of the flatback meat filled the kitchen, along with the smells of coffee and freshly-baked bread. Stevo was seated at the table, dressed for the day, as usual reading the newspapers when Josef entered.

"Dobro jutro." greeted Stevo. "Did you sleep well?"

"Dobro jutro." replied Josef, smiling at Ignatz, nodding to the offered cup of coffee. He was also dressed, but no tie. "I may have slept better, if I didn't spend most of the night waiting to hear Barbra cry."

Stevo nodded, "Yes, I was listening, but didn't hear anything."

Just then, Barbra appeared, smelling of roses from bathing with her scented soap. She wore a morning robe of peach-colored satin, embroidered with white flowers. Her damp hair was piled atop her head. She looked fresh and rested. Both men rose when she entered the room. She acknowledged them with a dazzling smile. "Good morning." she said, taking the chair Ignatz held out for her. He was back instantly with coffee prepared just as she liked it. She heard the meat sizzling and the aroma filled the kitchen. She said, "Ignatz, whatever you are cooking smells wonderful." Stevo and Josef exchanged puzzled looks. They each had expected Barbra to be distraught by Stefan's ignoring her at the Gary Hotel and most of all, by not returning last night.

Barbra placed a napkin on her lap. Seeing both men openly staring at her, she said, "What is the matter? Do I have something on my face?"

Josef, his face serious, said, "Yes, something is the matter. How is it you are so cheerful? For more than a year I have seen you in different stages of depression. Today, when I expected you to be distraught, you are anything but that. You…you look absolutely calm and almost pleased."

With a self-satisfied look, her eyes went from Stevo to Josef. "Well," she said, "I have made plans for my future." The look of bewilderment on both men's faces made her laugh…that musical laugh that men found so attractive.

Ignatz, also listening, placed a plate of meat in front of Barbra, before serving the men.

Josef, as Barbra's doctor, knew her very well. He wondered if this behavior was a prelude to possible hysterics. Barbra, seeing the troubled look in Josef's eyes, said, "Don't worry, Josef. There won't be any more crying. I know what I want to do." Ignatz, standing next to Barbra, along with the seated Stevo and Josef, stared openly at Barbra.

Josef ran his fingers through his dark hair, not sure what to say or ask. After what seemed like a long pause, he said, "You find that your husband is with another woman and you have just lost your Papa." Again he paused, looking for the right words. "After all, you are in mourning for your father."

"No." said Barbra firmly. "I will not wear black, not even an arm band."

Ignatz's mouth dropped open, while Stevo's and Josef 's eyes widened in wonder.

"You aren't going to observe the year's mourning for your Papa?" asked a stunned Josef. She looked confidently at Josef and then to Stevo. "I spent most of the night thinking." she said. "I spoke to my Papa as if he were in the room with me. I told him I was finished with mourning and crying. I spent over a year crying for my dead babies. There are no more tears left to shed."

When neither man replied to her statement, she went on. "I even thought about returning to Europe, but changed my mind. Germany and Zagreb are my past." Again she looked to the men for some reaction, seeing none, she said, "America is a new start for me. Perhaps there are opportunities for me here I haven't thought of." Stevo said nothing, only looked with admiration at this strong, German woman. Josef asked, "What about Stefan?" Barbra turned her attention to Stevo, saying, "When Stefan returns, I will need to find another place to live.

You see," she said with conviction, "as of yesterday, I no longer consider him my husband. By the company I saw him with he must not consider himself my husband."

Stevo didn't realize he had been holding his breath. He let out his breath before saying, "I would hate to see you leave." He turned to Josef, "I mean that for you also. In less than a day, I have become fond of both of you." Stevo glanced at Ignatz who was smiling broadly. "I think Ignatz would like for you to stay." he said.

Barbra, smiling, picked up her knife and fork and attacked the food on her plate, saying, "That is settled. I am no longer married. I will no longer be in mourning. I have you two and Ignatz as my friends and protectors."

At that moment, Tomo and Marjan exited their room at the far end of the kitchen.

Tomo said, "Forgive us. We didn't want to interrupt your conversation. We heard it all." He looked at Barbra. "We would also like to be your friends and protectors."

Before Barbra could reply, a knock sounded at the door. A tall bearded man wearing a flat cap and work clothes asked for Barbra Vladeslav.

Ignatz showed the man in. Barbra didn't rise, but turned to face the man. Through the open door she could see a large horse drawn wagon in the yard.

With his cap in his hands, the man said nervously, "Count Vladeslav asked me to come for his belongings."

Barbra said nothing, staring at the man who nervously twisted his cap in his hands.

After a long pause, she rose from her seat saying, "Come Ignatz, let's pack Stefan's things." To the tall man she said, "You may wait outside."

Upstairs, Barbra opened Stefan's steamer trunk, preparing to place his shirts and socks in the drawers. Ignatz was already hanging trousers and jackets on the clothes rack provided on the other side of the trunk.

When Barbra pulled open the drawer of a small side table, she caught her breath. There was only one item in the drawer, a red velvet box. She recognized the box. *How was it she didn't miss it when she packed to come to America?*

She slowly opened the lid of the square box. Tears blurred her vision as she looked at the jewels inside. The parure, as the French called it, was the matching set of Czechoslovakian garnets. The box was custom made to hold the stunning necklace of five large garnets encircled with smaller round ones ending in dangles of tear drop stones. The matching bracelet was nestled in its own place as were the chandelier earrings. Above the necklace rested the brooch.

Barbra never thought Stefan would stoop so low as to steal her Mutti's jewels, a wedding gift from Papa to Mutti on their wedding day.

With her sleeve, Barbra brushed aside the tears. She put the box of garnets under her pillow. Ignatz, watching her, was concerned. He had never before seen this angry expression on her face.

Barbra stood looking around the room. The only piece of luggage small enough for her to carry was the leather man's hat box. Seeing it, she grabbed it by the strap and ran toward the stairs. With all her might, she flung the round box down the stairs where it slid, bounced, and landed with a loud thud.

Above the bouncing and thudding, Stevo and Josef heard Barbra shout, "Ich konnti ihn töten".

Startled by the noise, the four men in the kitchen ran through the door leading to the store. They saw the bruised leather hat box resting at the base of the stairs. Looking up, they saw a defiant Barbra, her hands on her hips.

Stevo said to Josef, "I don't understand German. Do you know what she said?"

Josef paused a moment, thinking, "I studied German in school. I think she wants to kill someone."

Ignatz appeared at her side, calling down to Tomo and Marjan, "I need some help with the trunk and suitcase."

Both young men hurried up to help. Being young and strong, they easily carried the steamer trunk down the stairs and out to the wagon. Ignatz scooted the large leather suitcase half the way down a step at a time. Tomo appeared, taking the suitcase and putting it in the wagon alongside the trunk.

Barbra appeared in the doorway, now very calm. "That is all we have for you."

The driver of the wagon, still with his hat in his hand, appeared confused. "I was told there would me much more."

Barbra said, cooly, "If Stefan Vladeslav thinks there is more belonging to him, tell him to come and get it himself."

CHAPTER 8

It was the middle of the week about six in the evening. Milan's tavern was lively with music and customers. Some were neatly dressed, while others were in their soiled mill clothes. Seeing the men dressed in their mill clothes offended no one.

Ivanka was a now a familiar sight and everyone appeared to like her. Most of the men sensed that she was off limits and no one grabbed at her or said anything that might have offended her, or for that matter, angering Milan or his brother, Mato.

Ivanka was warm and friendly and enjoyed working at the tavern. The men joked with her and complimented her, which she liked. She slept in the unfinished house behind the tavern, made comfortable with a goose down quilt.

Milan came alongside Ivanka, dressed in the green scoop neck blouse and gathered skirt that was once Katya's. He nodded towards the doorway at the men entering. One of the men was Stanko Perpich. Milan warned Ivanka, "Stanko is a customer. You had better forget that he was once important to you." Milan gave Ivanka a stern look saying, "Don't cause any trouble here. This is how Mato and I make a living." Squeezing her arm he said, "Remember that!"

Ivanka said nothing. She watched as Stanko and the three men he came with found a nearby table. To Milan's horror, she headed straight for that table.

"Pivo, slivovitza?" she asked, smiling at the men. Almost all the men in the bar had heard of the slap Ivanka gave Stanko, so the room went quiet while everyone stared at the table. Stanko did not look at Ivanka. One of the other men, cleared his throat and said, "Pivo, beer for all of us."

"Ceteri pivo…four beers." she said and went to the bar for the tray of beers.

Milan poured the beers into mugs, all the while watching Ivanka, who innocently looked back at him. When the filled mugs were on the tray, Ivanka picked it up giving Milan a wink.

Oh shit. What is she up to?

Ivanka set the tray on the table and placed a beer mug in front of each man. Stanko still did not look at her. She never lost her smile, which became larger when one of the men paid her and told her not to bring any change.

Back at the bar, Ivanka placed the tray on it. Fighting to hide a smile, Milan looked at her with narrowing eyes saying, "So, you think you can play with me?" She smiled at him with a twinkle in her eye, saying, "I just did!"

At the sound of the door opening, almost all the customers near the bar turned to look at the group of people entering the tavern. Stevo held open the door for Barbra, followed by Josef and then Tomo, and Marjan.

There was a momentary hush as the patrons looked at the new arrivals…the novo doshli.

For just a second, Milan felt light-headed. Seeing Stevo with a red-headed woman brought back memories of Katya. Of course he realized it wasn't Katya, but seeing Barbra enter with Stevo left him a bit rattled. Milan left his place from behind the bar and greeted Stevo with, "Well, it is about time you came to visit." He then turned his gaze to Barbra. *She's beautiful, but doesn't look anything like Katya*, he thought to himself.

Stevo introduced Barbra, hatless, dressed in a slender blue dress, to Milan, saying, "This is Milan, the owner of this tavern and one of my closest friends." To Milan, he said, "This is Barbra Vladeslav." Milan showed no surprise or recognition of the name, as he took Barbra's hand and touched it to his lips. "We are honored to have you come to our simple little tavern."

Stevo wondered when Milan had become such a gracious host. "This is Doctor Josef Popovich." said Stevo. Milan extended his hand smiling, while thinking, *a handsome, blue-eyed Doctor, won't the women be happy.*

A few men who knew Stevo came to greet him and hoped they would be introduced to the newcomers. Barbra smiled graciously, touched by all the attention she and Josef were getting. The crowd around them got larger with hand shaking and offers of drinks, until Milan said, "Come, I have a table for you."

Ivanka had already wiped clean a table and slapped the chair seats with the towel to give them a quick cleaning.

Only Stevo, Josef, and Barbra came to the table. Tomo and Marjan stayed at the bar talking with friends. It wasn't long before both of them went to the back of room to be with the tamburashi…the musicians.

The room smelled of beer and liquor and the air was thick with cigarette smoke. Stevo looked at Barbra as she glanced around the room looking at the people. Thinking she might be disappointed, he said, "Perhaps for your first night out in Gary, I should have taken you a nicer place."

"Oh, no," said Barbra emphatically, "this reminds me of my uncle's tavern in Ilmenau, back in Germany. I almost grew up in his tavern."

Ivanka came for their orders, trying not to stare at Barbra, who asked, "What is your name?" Barbra's Croatian was pretty good, but with a definite German accent, which delighted the nearby eavesdroppers.

Shyly, the girl said, "Ivanka." With an extended hand, Barbra said, "I am Barbra." Awed, Ivanka shook Barbra's hand.

In all the time Josef had known Barbra, he had never seen this side of her. Her eyes scanned the room taking in all the people, reminding her of her childhood visits to Ilmenau. She was definitely pleased to be at Milan's.

Josef glanced towards the musicians when he heard the music start. He saw that Marjan was sitting among them with a borrowed brach, playing the song Kukavica. Tomo sang the words to the song in a beautiful tenor voice.

Agrli me i podji putem kuda idu kukavice
Pratice te moje oci lutalice
Zensko srce nezno poput lastavice
Sto od bola ugine
Zagrli me samo jednom covek budi, ne lazi me
Ako odes nikad vise, ne trazi me

Hug me and go off on the road of cowards
My wandering eyes will follow you
Female heart tender as a little martin (soft bird)
That dies of pain
Hug me, just for once be a man, don't lie to me
If you leave ever again, don't seek me

The conversations and loud laughter became quiet, as everyone listened to Tomo sing. He was still a favorite just as he had been when he first sang in the tavern nearly five years ago.

Josef, handsome in a brown suit and yellow tie, said with admiration, "Tomo is a wonderful singer." Nodding towards the people in the tavern he said, "Look at them. They are all listening and enjoying the song."

Stevo agreed, "Yes, for a while I thought he might take up singing with groups as a living. I am happy he stayed with me."

Barbra said nothing. She was enthralled with the music, with Tomo's singing and the camaraderie she felt in the room.

Ivanka delivered the drinks to the table along with an ashtray.

Josef left the table, going to the musicians. When he returned he didn't sit, but waited for the music to start. As soon as the strains of a waltz began, he held his hand out to Barbra saying, "We have never danced. May I have this waltz?"

Stevo wished he had thought of asking for a waltz. Milan appeared and sat in the empty chair next to him. Milan placed shot glasses of slivovitz in front of Stevo and himself.

"You could have warned me." he said, touching glasses with Stevo.

Stevo looked puzzled for only a moment saying, "Oh, the red hair."

"Not only the red hair, but the blue dress." Seeing that Stevo didn't understand, he went on, "The night I invited myself to go with you and Katya to the Orpheum Theatre to see the Petticoat Minstrals Burlesque. Remember she wore a blue lace dress?"

Stevo smiled at the memory of that night. He could have choked Milan for getting himself invited on that evening, but now…now…it was a wonderful memory. There were so many memories of the two men, great friends, rivals for the same woman.

For a while the two friends didn't talk, and just watched Josef and Barbra dance.

"Tell me," said Milan, his gaze was on the dance floor, watching Josef and Barbra, now the only dancers on the floor. The other dancers left the floor to watch the handsome couple as they twirled to the beauty of the waltz. "Barbra is a Vladeslav?"

Before Stevo could reply, the dance ended with applause as Josef was leading Barbra back to the table.

Seeing that Stevo had no time to talk, Milan said, "I will be visiting Katya tomorrow around noon. If you can come, we will talk then." By 'visiting' Katya, it meant that Milan would be making his regular trip to the cemetery where he always left a bouquet of flowers, drank some wine, and talked to the only woman he had ever loved.

"I'll be there." said Stevo, as Milan took the empty shot glasses leaving the table with a nod to Josef.

Josef held a chair for Barbra before sitting in his chair. Barbra pulled a handkerchief tucked into the wrist-length sleeve of her dress, wiping the drops of perspiration from her forehead saying, "That was lovely. I can't remember the last time I danced a waltz."

A man dressed in his mill work clothes, with a kerchief tied at his neck, came to Stevo's table. He looked at Barbra with admiration. Having been encouraged by his companions at the bar, he said, "I...we," he waived his hand towards the bar at the grinning men there, "want to tell you that you are the most beautiful woman we have ever seen."

Milan was on his way to hustle the man from the table, but stopped when Barbra stood. She turned towards the bar and bowed to the men who whooped and clapped.

The man backed away from the table with a huge grin, pleased and proud that he was brave enough to come to speak to the beautiful lady.

The music started again, with songs remembered from the old country and the buzzing of conversations filled the room.

It wasn't long before the tamburashi played a kolo, filling the floor with both men and women linking arms to do the circle dance. More applause broke out as Ivanka abandoned her serving tray on the bar and hurried to join the circle.

Milan looked on with wonder. Never had his tavern been filled with joy as he witnessed this evening. His face darkened as he saw Stanko Perpich break into the kolo circle to take Ivanka's hand. Milan saw the momentary look of displeasure on Ivanka's face, quickly replaced by relief when Milan's brother Mato broke into the circle taking Ivanka's hand.

There were whispers among the several customers who had witnessed or heard about the slap delivered to Stanko by Ivanka. Before the kolo ended, Stanko had dropped out of the dance, returning to his table.

This event at Milan's would be talked about for days. It was a night made for gossip.

Barbra watched as Ivanka returned to the bar to pick up her tray of beer. She had two trays for the same table. Milan was about to pick up the tray to assist her, when Barbra went to the bar. Stevo and Josef looked at one another not knowing what was about to happen. Barbra gave Ivanka a knowing look as she picked up three mugs in one hand and only two in the other.

With hands on her hips and a smile on her pretty face, Ivanka realized this was to be a friendly competition. She laughed out loud as she tried to pick up three mugs in one hand.

The men at the bar stared at the two women. Try as she might, Ivanka could not hold three mugs in one hand, so she held two in each.

Barbra with a mischievous look in her eye, nodded to Ivanka, who immediately understood this was to be a race to the table without spilling the beer.

Milan realized what was about to happen and thought to himself, *Oh, shit! Broken mugs and spilled beer on the floor.*

The patrons burst into applause as the race, with no spilled beer, ended in a tie. The laughing men at the table asked Barbra if she and Ivanka would race again.

Barbra shook her head no, putting her arm around Ivanka's shoulder.

A generous tip of a Barber quarter was put in Ivanka's hand and one in Barbra's. Barbra looked at the coin, smiled, nodded a thank you and handed it to Ivanka. Again, the watching patrons burst into applause.

Back at their table, Josef asked Barbra, "How did you know you could do that without spilling the beer, or for that matter, not dropping a mug?"

Barbra smiled, remembering her time at her Uncle Fritz's tavern, saying my cousin, Cristal, and I would have races like this often when I visited there. But I noticed something tonight." She paused and looked at her left hand, "I can hold three mugs with my right hand, but I can no longer lift three with my left hand."

At the door, Bobo stepped into the tavern. He stayed at the door, waiting until he caught Milan's attention. Milan nodded and went to Stevo' table. He said, "Bobo is here. Are you ready to leave?"

Stevo put some money on the table saying, "We had better go before you take Barbra away from us. She and Ivanka would make a good team for your business."

Tomo and Marjan waved goodbye to the trio as they weren't ready to leave.

Bobo, as always, stopped the carriage as close to the kitchen door as he could.

It pleased Bobo to hear laughter and happy conversations once again. Since Katya's death, the atmosphere was quiet…solemn…lonely.

Stevo helped Barbra from the carriage and she went directly to the door. "Oh, look!" she cried out. "What is this?" She knelt and took into her arms a pitiful looking dog. Standing up she showed it to Josef and Stevo saying, "Look at his poor little face. He has a scar. Oh, and his ear has been torn."

Josef laughed saying, "He is cute in a scruffy way."

Stevo took Mali from Barbra's arms saying to the dog, "So, you have decided to come home."

Ignatz heard the carriage and was holding the door open for them. He was surprised to see Mali.

Once inside, Stevo explained Mali had been Katya's pet. "I didn't want him. He was all beaten up when she brought him home. She and Cleona nursed him to health." Stevo nuzzled Mali's head saying, "It wasn't long before we all fell in love with him. Recently Mali moved out, going to live with Bobo in the barn.

Ignatz was the only one who knew why Mali had left the house for the barn. Ignatz saw Stefan kick Mali when the little dog wandered into Stefan's room. Mali had let out a yelp, limped down the stairs and went directly to the safety and comforting friendship of Bobo.

CHAPTER 9

It was a bit past noon when Bobo, driving the single buggy, dropped Stevo off very near the cemetery in Tolleston. "Don't bother waiting. I will walk back." said Stevo.

Stevo walked through the grass, careful not to step on any of the graves as it was known to bring bad luck.

He saw Milan wearing a brimmed hat to shade his eyes, sitting on the ground with his back leaning against the side of Katya's grave stone. Milan heard him coming. "I was watching for you." he said. "Come sit. The grass is dry."

Before Stevo sat, he kissed his fingertips then touched the marble headstone.

Once Stevo was seated cross-legged, Milan offered him the wine bottle. Stevo took a drink from the bottle noticing the fresh-cut flowers on the grave. The patrons of Milan's Tavern would never guess there was a tender side to this big tough man who was known to pick up men and bodily throw them out of the bar when trouble started.

Katya's head stone was next to Ivan Balaban's stone, but no mention of her marriage to him was indicated on either stone.

"Tell me," said Milan, "how is it that Barbra is a Vladeslav?"

With a small shake of his head, as if he couldn't believe it himself, Stevo said, "She is Stefan's wife."

Milan turned towards Stevo somewhat surprised saying, "And he let her come to my place with the two of you? If Barbra were my wife, I would have been there with her."

"Well," continued Stevo, "Stefan saw Barbra at the Gary Hotel, where she and Josef were waiting for me." Stevo paused for effect, "When he saw Barbra, he was with another woman and totally ignored her."

Milan leaned up on one elbow, totally surprised by this news asked, "What did Barbra do…say?"

"Nothing," answered Stevo, "she just turned and got into the carriage."

Swatting at an annoying fly Milan said, "If it had been Ivanka, there probably would have been a fight." Then he pressed on, "Really? She didn't say anything?"

"Not a word. Her expression didn't indicate she knew him." Now the fly was buzzing at Stevo's face. "And," he continued, "we haven't seen Stefan since that night. He hasn't come to his room at my place."

Milan said nothing, shaking his head in disbelief. He took the wine bottle from Stevo and took a long drink. "There is no way I would ignore such a woman." he said.

"Oh, and… "Stevo said, knowing what he was going to say next would really set Milan off, "Stefan sent a man with a wagon for his possessions."

Now Milan sat up straight, "Vrag, the devil. What the hell!" he said.

Stevo was almost laughing for he knew Milan so well and expected this reaction. "You should have been there." said Stevo. "Barbra threw down the stairs the only case she could lift, shouting something in German. Josef thinks she said she wants to kill Stefan."

Milan, still holding onto the wine bottle, took another long drink. Handing the bottle back to Stevo, he said, "Maika Boze…Holy Mary."

Stevo said, "The man who came for Stefan's things came with a large wagon, thinking there would be more than the trunks and suitcases. Obviously Stefan wanted the pictures and sculptures he had in my store."

Milan's eyes were wide with interest. "So…" he prompted Stevo to hurry with his story.

Stevo said, "Barbra told the man with the wagon if Mr. Vladeslav wanted anything else, he should come for it himself." Stevo lifted his hands palms outward, saying, "Stefan hasn't been back or called."

Both men were silent for a while, lost in their thoughts. After a while, Milan rolled over on his knees, holding onto the stone to get up more easily. This maneuver surprised Stevo, for Milan had always been so strong and muscular.

Milan saw the look on Stevo's face saying, "I guess I'm getting old."

The two friends walked slowly down the road they had traveled many times. When they reached Milan's tavern, Stevo said, "I better get back to the store. I left Tomo in charge."

Stevo entered through the back gate behind the store. He noticed the large, enclosed wagon was gone. Bobo saw Stevo and hurried from the barn. "Tomo and Marjan took the store wagon with some coffins to the mill hospital." he said.

"Is the store closed?" asked Stevo.

"No, Miss Barbra and the doctor said they would take care of the store." said Bobo wiping his soiled hands with a rag.

Stevo nodded to Bobo, thinking *Oh, God do they know what they are doing?* Once in the kitchen, he went directly to the opposite door into the store.

The first thing he noticed were some pieces of paper, folded tent-like on three items with the word SOLD in bold letters printed on them. He saw Barbra dressed in a cream colored dress with a matching lace blouse. At her neck was a long gold chain from which hung a large gold oval locket.

Barbra was at the door shaking hands with a man who smiled warmly at her. He didn't wear a suit jacket or a tie, but was cleanly dressed in dark trousers and a white shirt with brown stripes. He looked very nice. His wife wore a peasant skirt and long-sleeved blouse in a blue floral print.

Stevo saw Barbra hold her hand up, to stop the couple from leaving the store. At a nearby table, Barbra picked up a small figurine. She hurried to the woman and handed it to her. The woman's face broke into a smile when she realized the figurine was a gift from Barbra. The husband again took Barbra's hand, shaking it once more with a big smile.

Barbra stood at the door, waving and calling a "Thank you." to them as they walked away smiling.

Turning away from the door, Barbra saw Stevo near the back of the room. She smiled, calling out, "You are back so soon."

Next to the kitchen door was the desk used for recording business transactions. Doctor Josef was seated there, with a ledger opened before him. Under the desk was Mali, just as he always stayed when Stevo was seated there. Looking up Josef said, "I think I entered the sales correctly. You will have to check and see what I have entered."

Stevo took the ledger with its alphabetical tabs looking at the page Josef pointed to.

Josef said, "Please don't think I was invading your privacy when looking at some of the pages, I only wanted to see how I should enter the sales and the payments made."

Scanning the page, Stevo said, "This is exactly how I would have posted it."

"Look under the L's. We had another sale there. Paid in cash, but will pick up tomorrow. I wrote out a receipt." Josef pointed to the entry.

Barbra looking very pleased said, "I enjoyed myself today. I felt useful."

Stevo looked from Josef to Barbra with a certain amount of admiration. He said, "You both surprise and please me. It is as if you both have worked here for months."

Josef said, "When Tomo and Marjan had to leave, Barbra and I couldn't see closing the store." The doctor looked into Stevo's face for a reaction saying, "I hope we didn't overstep ourselves.

"Not at all, Mnogo Hvala...many thanks." said Stevo. "Actually, I am pleased to know that when needed, you two might be available." He turned to Barbra asking, "What did you give the woman as she was leaving?"

"Oh, that. Just an unimportant figurine from the things Stefan had brought here." As she spoke, she tore a sheet of paper in half, writing SOLD on it.

She walked to the wall of paintings and tucked the paper with SOLD written on it between the frame and canvas.

"You sold a painting?" asked a very surprised Stevo.

"No." said Barbra, "I plan to keep this for myself. But, it doesn't hurt to have a sold sign on it for a couple of months, perhaps to show customers you have some art lovers coming here."

Stevo walked through his store noticing some very nice re-arranging had been done. He asked, "Did you two do this?"

Josef said, "I hope you don't mind. Again he said, we didn't mean to overstep ourselves." He paused a moment studying Stevo's face. "You see," he went on, "we had some time on our hands."

"Let's go into the kitchen." said Stevo.

Josef said, "If you don't mind, Mali and I will stay in the store. I can call you when someone comes in."

Ignatz had some salami and cheese slices along with fresh sliced cucumbers on the table.

Barbra sat opposite Stevo, putting a napkin on her lap. She said to Ignatz, "Just some cold water to drink."

From the wooden, double door, steel-lined Seroco ice-cooled refrigerator, Ignatz removed a water pitcher. He poured a glass for Barbra. When he saw a nod from Stevo, he filled another glass.

Before Barbra and Stevo finished their lunch, they heard the sound of a bell attached to the top of the door, signaling someone had entered the store.

Milan's brother Mato, holding Ivanka's elbow, guided her into the store.

Ivanka was in awe of all the lovely furnishings on display. She had never seen such tables, chairs or cabinets. In her home in Strašnik she only saw wooden benches and wooden slab tables.

Barbra was the first through the door, smiling broadly at Ivanka, who wore a white skirt and blouse with red floral appliqué trimming. It was one of the two outfits Stevo gave to Milan for Ivanka. Behind Barbra was Stevo. Josef, seated at the desk at the back of the store, rose when he saw Mato and Ivanka.

"Zdravo…welcome." said Stevo, offering his hand to Mato. "What brings you here?"

Josef waived a greeting to Mato while Barbra put a friendly arm around Ivanka.

Mato said, "We need curtains for the new house in back of the tavern. Ivanka was going to sew them by hand." He rolled his eyes and shook his head, "That would take forever. We are here to buy a sewing machine."

Barbra pulled Ivanka towards the east wall of the store where several sewing machines were in a row. "Do you want one with a cabinet or just a machine with drawers?" asked Barbra.

Ivanka had no idea what Barbra was talking about. She had never seen a sewing machine and was sure she would never be able to use one. Ivanka's head was in a whirl as Barbra showed her the New Queen $11 oak, four-drawer, drop-head pedal machine. The Burdick $13.85 oak, six-drawer pedal machine had a wooden cover to place over the sewing machine. The most expensive and beautiful of all the machines was the $23.20 Minnesota cabinet machine. When the machine was dropped down, a marble-topped flat lid made the cabinet look like a lovely piece of furniture. When closed, the two drawers and foot pedal were hidden behind ornately carved doors.

Mato asked Ivanka, "Which do you like?"

Ivanka's eyes were wide. She was embarrassed. The girl had no idea what to do with these machines.

The door bell sounded and in walked Cleona, Bobo's cousin and Katya's business partner before Katya became ill. Mali came running from his resting place beneath the desk where Josef worked.

Stopping only a moment to pet the dog, Cleona walked up to the small group gathered around the sewing machines. She said, "Hello, Mr. Steve, she nodded a greeting to Mato. Did I come at a bad time? Looks like you have a lot of customers. I'll just go wait in the kitchen."

"No." said Stevo. "This is Ivanka she works for Mato and Milan. And this is Barbra Vladeslav, just arrived from Europe."

Cleona looked at the beautiful woman with red hair and smiled saying "Happy to meet you Miss Barbra."

Thinking Barbra was purchasing the sewing machine, she said in her limited Croatian, "I know the fancy cabinet is the best sewing machine."

Mato said, "Then that is the one we will take." He looked at Ivanka who was flushed with embarrassment. "What is the matter?" he asked her.

The girl was almost in tears as she said softly, "I don't know what to do with this machine. I can only sew by hand."

Cleona put an arm around Ivanka's shoulders. She said, "Milan and Mato are old and good friends of mine. In fact, I still have Milan's goats in my yard." Cleona looked at Mato, saying, "Let me know when the machine is at your place. I will come by and teach this girl how to use it." She turned to Ivanka, who didn't know what to think of this black woman and heard Cleona ask, "Is that alright with you, Miss Ivanka?"

CHAPTER 10

Stevo walked out the front of the store with Mato and Ivanka, where they stood chatting for a while.

At the yard entrance, Tomo and Marjan pulled in past the kitchen closer to the barn. Marjan stayed with Bobo to unhitch the horse and put the enclosed wagon away.

Barbra and Cleona were sitting in the kitchen, watching a smiling Ignatz stretch pieces of dough not larger than the palm of his hand which he then dropped into a pot of hot cooking grease. The room smelled wonderful. When several krustule were done frying, he put them on a plate, sprinkling generously with sugar.

A stack of napkins was already on the table. Ignatz placed the plate of krustule in the center of them. There were no forks as usually these were hand held, and sometimes pulled apart into smaller pieces.

He warned, "Wait a bit for them to cool."

Cleona, sitting next to Barbra said, "You smell of roses. Are you wearing scented rose water?"

"No," said Barbra, shooing a persistent fly buzzing away from the plate. "It must be my rose soap you smell. I only have part of one soap cake left."

Cleona, now very interested, asked, "You buy that here in Gary?"

Carefully picking up a krustule, Barbra said, "Oh, no. I haven't been anywhere but to Milan's. I brought the soap from Germany."

Cleona picked up her black satchel and put it on the lap of her blue full skirt. She reached in pulling out a bar of her Royal Honey Soap saying, "I make soap." She handed it to Barbra, who put down her fried cake and admired the bar wrapped in white cloth tied with what had become the Royal trademark, a pink ribbon.

Impressed, Barbra raised the soap to smell it. "This is lovely." she said.

Just then Tomo walked in. Overhearing the conversation, he came to the table and sat down with a huge smile. He patted Cleona's hand affectionately. Back when he first met her and she was hired to take care of the ill Katya after the death of her first husband Ivan, Tomo was almost afraid of the bossy black woman.

He said proudly, "Show Barbra what else you make. I know you have it with you. You always do."

Smiling a bit sheepishly, Cleona reached into her bag and pulled out first, the bottle of Royal Witch Hazel, with its wax-covered cork, tied with a pink ribbon. Next came the jar of Honey Face Cream, this with a larger wax-covered cork and tied with a pink ribbon.

Tomo reached for a krustule just as Ignatz refilled the plate. With a mouth full of delicious sweet fried dough, Tomo said, "I am the reason Cleona and Katya started making the Honey Cream."

Barbra's eyes got wide. "You?" she asked.

Cleona admonished Tomo, as if he were still the 15-year-old boy she knew when she met him, "Don't be talkin with your mouth full." She turned to Barbra, "This boy got hisself beat up real bad by some men at Milan's. It's a long story and it doesn't matter why. Well, yes it does matter. The men came to beat up Milan and said something about Katya." Cleona paused in her story and looked warmly at Tomo. "This boy tried to defend Katya's name and got such a beating we thought he would die or his face be scarred forever."

Tomo interrupted, "I was sleeping upstairs in the loft, where Igantz sleeps now. Katya and Cleona put cool towels on my face along with witch hazel and then kept me lathered in fresh honey." He smiled, took another bite of the crispy fried cake, waiting for effect. He swallowed and said, "After two weeks, Cleona and Katya decided my skin was pretty." Laughing he said, "Now is that any way to compliment a man? Say he is pretty?"

Cleona pursed her lips and shook her head at Tomo, as if he were a child. To Barbra she said, "That was when we got the idea for the cream. I was living in Katya's house, sleeping on the back porch. I cooked here and we ate here because we done turned the kitchen in her house into our place of business.

Both Stevo and Josef, unnoticed, had been standing at the kitchen door leading into the store. Trying to sound annoyed, Stevo announced, "They didn't only eat here, but melted their wax and pasted their labels at the very table where you are sitting."

To Tomo, Stevo said, "Come in here when you are finished eating, and tell me about this morning." To Josef, he said, "Would you care to stay to learn more about the fees and what took place?"

Pleased to be included, Josef stepped into the kitchen, grinning sheepishly as he grabbed a krustule, paused a moment, and took a second one with him into the store. Tomo said to Barbra and Cleona, "I must go."

Ignatz, with a plate of more fried cakes said, "I am going to the barn to give these to Bobo and Marjan.

Barbra and Cleona were alone in the kitchen. Both women were quiet, each thinking about the same thing. Barbra was the first to speak. "Do you think you could make rose soap?"

Cleona grinned with her white toothed smile, "I been thinking the same thing. Do I need fresh roses?"

Barbra thought a moment, then said, "I think you could use rose oil, if you can find it." Barbra rose from her chair going to the open doorway into the store. She motioned to Josef, catching his eye. He came quickly. She asked, "Is rose oil something I could find in an apotecka…pharmacy?"

Before he could ask why the question, Stevo called him back. Quickly Josef said, "I would think you could find it there."

In the store, the three men sat at a nearby table, careful not to scratch it for it was merchandise. Josef didn't have a napkin, so he used his handkerchief to keep the loose sugar from landing on the table top.

Tomo pulled from his pocket a piece of paper. Showing it to Stevo, he said, "I had quite a time getting the foreman to sign this. He claims he never paid this much for caskets in the past."

Taking the paper from Tomo, Stevo looked over the figures saying, "This is what we have always charged. Do you suppose they are getting caskets from another seller?"

"I don't know who that would be." said Tomo.

The men were silent as Stevo studied the paper and the signature. Tomo broke the silence saying, "Marjan is in love."

Both Josef and Stevo looked at Tomo. Stevo said, "We know about Ivanka."

With an *I know something you don't* look on his face, Tomo said, "It isn't Ivanka anymore."

The two men showed some surprise and interest. Before they could ask who, Tomo said, "After the bodies were put in the caskets only one was not picked up by family. We went to Van Buren Street to a really small place. Most of the places were just a little more than large sheds. When we got to the two room house, we saw the mother, who started crying when she saw us. With her were two older daughters and two small sons. We were bringing home her oldest son who worked at the mill where his father also works.

I understood that the family was new to Gary. They are Slovaks so we were able to understand each other. The oldest daughter, Julia, pulled a bench from the table and we put the casket on it. There was no where else to put it."

"Well," said Josef, "Marjan is in love, so who is he in love with?"

Laughing softly and shaking his head in wonder, Tomo said, "He took one look at the younger sister, I think her name was Mara, and that was it." He slapped his hand on the table top with emphasis repeating, "And that was it!"

In the kitchen, Barbra and Cleona were excitedly planning the possibility of making rose-scented soap. Cleona was concerned with the making of the soap, while Barbra's artistic nature was towards the presentation of the soap. She didn't see it in the usual pink package. She wanted something more dramatic.

Barbra turned to Cleona, who was staring into space, lost in the planning of the new soap line. "What if," said Barbra, "we wrapped the rose soap in a rose-colored fabric?"

Sensing Cleona was not completely sold on the idea, Barbra added, "We could tie it with a rose colored ribbon instead of the pink you use now."

Cleona said, "First let me see if I can make a good bar of rose soap. Then we got to find just the right fabric, one that suits the soap."

Barbra nodded, understanding Cleona. Before she could say anything, Stevo and Josef entered the kitchen. Josef was looking for more of the fried cakes. He picked up a cooled one from the plate.

Back from the barn, the ever-attentive Ignatz, wearing his usual black waiter-type apron, brought a pitcher of cold water and a bottle of wine to the table. He disappeared to gather up some glasses.

Josef said, "This has been an eventful day. I rather enjoyed all the activity. Is it always like this?" he asked, pouring wine for Stevo and himself. He held up the wine bottle offering it to the women, who shook their heads no. He then poured the cold water in their glasses, before touching his wine glass.

He raised his wine glass to Cleona in a touching toast to the woman, "To my and Barbra's new friend."

The little black woman, usually so bossy and blustery, was so touched she just looked wide-eyed at the glasses raised in her honor.

"Mr. Steve," she said. "I don't know what to say. What am I supposed to say?"

Stevo smiled. Cleona was part of the family. She took care of Katya when his bride was dying. He said, "Just smile, Cleona, and say thank you."

With a catch in her throat, Cleona said, "Thank you, all." She didn't see Ignatz behind her, with his glass raised in his toast to her.

A bit embarrassed and not sure how to react to all the attention given her, Cleona said, "I suppose I should get back to the house and see how the girl is doin boilin the witch hazel bark. Sometimes these new girls don't cook it long enough."

Cleona stood, took Barbra's hand saying, "Thank you, Miss Barbra for givin me a new idea." She turned to Stevo and Josef smiling, "I thank you for bein such good friends."

When she was gone, the three sat silently at the table,each thinking over the events of the day. Stevo motioned for Ignatz to come join them at the table. The man only shook his head, following the dog, Mali, out into the yard.

Stevo looked long at Barbra. She looked back at him, a little confused at his stare. He said, "Barbra, I would like to take you out to downtown Gary this evening. Would you care to come?"

"We would love that." said Barbra, with a wide smile, her eyes sparkling.

Josef saw the fleeting look of disappointment flash across Stevo's face. Before Stevo could say anything, Josef said, "I don't think I want to go out tonight. Today has been so interesting, I think I will stay and look around the store and see what more I can learn about what we have to sell."

Barbra frowned saying, "Are you sure? It sounds like an adventure. We haven't really seen Gary."

"No," said Josef, "You two go. I think I will look around the store. If I am going to help in the store, I should know what we have. Maybe Tomo can help me if he has time.

CHAPTER 11

The next morning, Josef was already at the kitchen table, looking at the printed brochure from a Grand Rapids Michigan furniture manufacturer. The store had a few pieces from this company and Josef liked knowing the description of the workmanship and the woods used.

Barbra appeared smelling as always, of roses. She wore a loose-fitting peach-colored camisole top over a slim skirt, slightly flared at the hem. A long strand of pearls, looped twice, hung from her neck. On her ears were small matching pearl earrings.

She touched Josef's shoulder lightly with her hand as she passed him to go to her usual chair. He looked up at her with his blue eyes, a smile on his lips.

"You look pleased." he said. "Was last night pleasant?"

Pouring Barbra's coffee, Ignatz gave a good morning nod.

Barbra looked at Josef over the cup of coffee as she sipped the hot liquid. Placing her cup on the table she said, "Oh Josef! It was so much fun. Such nicely dressed people and so many of them knew Stevo. He introduced me to almost everyone who greeted us."

Her eyes shined as she said, "We stopped at a place where people were looking into machines. I looked in one and it was what is called a movie. There was no talking, just movement. The one I watched was *Yellowstone Park Hold-Up*. We must go sometime." she said, "I think you would find it interesting." After another sip of coffee, with Ignatz listening nearby, she went on, "We stopped at a delightful little café for a glass of wine and then we went to the Orpheum Theatre where we saw what is called vaudeville. There were exotic dancers, singers, jugglers and even some women with very little clothing. Stevo thought I would be shocked, but I wasn't."

Ignatz refilled Josef's coffee cup. After taking a sip, Josef said, "I am glad you enjoyed yourself." His handsome face did not betray any disappointment, though he was jealous that Stevo had given Barbra such an enjoyable evening. He wished he could make Barbra that happy.

Without knocking, Cleona came excitedly through the door. "Miss Barbra," she said, "Look at this." In her hand she had a piece of fabric less than one half yard long. "Look at this pattern. What do you think?"

Barbra rose and the two women went to the open door for better light to look at the fabric. It was cotton with small red and pink roses clustered together with an occasional green leaf among the flowers.

"Oh, I like this." said Barbra. "Where did you get this? Can we get more?"

Still standing in the open doorway, Cleona said, "The junk man. He comes by every so often and rings his bell for me to come out and see what he got new. Missy and I would find all kinds of things we could use."

"Come sit." said Barbra motioning for Cleona to come to the table.

Again, Barbra asked, "Does he have more of this fabric?"

Cleona smiled at Ignatz and declined his offer of coffee, saying, "No, he ain't got anymore of this cloth, but he told me where he got it. He got it from a lady in downtown Gary. Here is her address." Scrawled in poor handwriting was the name Grace Adams and an address on the north side of Gary.

Tomo was just coming out of the bedroom at the far end of the kitchen when he heard Barbra read the name, Grace Adams.

Seeing him, Cleona said mischievously, "Maybe Tomo could take you there."

Cleona remembered that Tomo dated Grace Adams for a while and that it annoyed Katya that he would come home late in the night or a few times at daybreak, smelling of lilacs, Grace Adam's favorite scent.

With a towel draped around his neck, Tomo gave Cleona a playful squint eyed look saying, "I would love to take her there, but Stevo has my day planned for me. I am sure Bobo can take her there."

Tomo and Grace's romance faded in time, but it lasted long enough to annoy Katya who, before marrying Stevo, watched Grace and Adele Manning take up the time of the two men Katya considered as hers.

With just a touch of sarcasm in her voice, which Barbra noticed, Cleona said, "You be sure and tell Bobo how to find her house."

Wearing a summer straw hat, tied with a peach colored scarf matching her dress, Bobo helped Barbra from the fringe-trimmed buggy. Barbra looked at the nice houses and the well-kept lawns and marveled at the contrast of this area and The Patch where the mill workers lived.

Bobo walked her to the door. Once she rang the bell, he went back to the buggy.

Barbra rang again. An attractive woman answered the door. The first thing Barbra thought when she saw the woman was her beautiful dress. The silver grey chiffon dress complimented her light brown hair and hazel eyes. Barbra suspected the lovely complexion was aided with cosmetics.

"Yes?" said Grace. "May I help you?"

Barbra held up the piece of fabric Cleona had given her saying, "I was told I could get more of this fabric from you."

Slightly confused, Grace moved aside saying, "Please come in. I do have almost a full bolt of that fabric. She indicated with a motion of her hand that Barbra be seated on a satin-tufted striped settee.

Sitting across from Barbra in a matching striped chair, Grace asked, "Do you want me to make something for you with the fabric."

When Barbra looked confused, Grace said, "I am a seamstress. Isn't that why you are here?"

Barbra looked around the beautifully decorated room. There was an air of elegance to all the furnishings.

Grace asked, "How is it you knew I had this fabric?"

"The junk man gave it to a friend of mine." said Barbra, glancing around noticing the vases of beautiful flowers.

Grace said, "I planned to make a summer dress with the material, but it really is too distracting and busy to wear. It would work better as a table cloth and napkins or even a window curtain." She rose from her chair, "Excuse me while I get the fabric for you."

Barbra again looked around the room. The sunlight sparkled through the clean windows and seemed to illuminate all the shiny fabrics in the room. The air smelled lovely from the flowers displayed in crystal vases throughout the room.

Returning with the brightly colored bolt of fabric, Grace said, "Here is the fabric." Handing it to Barbra she asked, "May I get you some tea or coffee, Miss...Miss?"

"I am sorry." Apologized Barbra in her delightful accented English. "I am Barbra Vladeslav. I can't help but admire all the lovely flowers you have in the room."

Grace Adams stood staring at Barbra for a long moment. Barbra noticed the stare and felt a bit uncomfortable.

Grace asked, "Do you know the Count Vladeslav?"

Barbra blinked noticeably, but said nothing. *How did this woman know Stefan?*

Seeing the strange look on Barbra's face, Grace wasn't sure what to say, so she prattled on nervously, "The flowers were from the wedding of the Count and Adele Manning. I took the flowers when they left for their honeymoon in the East."

Barbra was stunned. *Stefan got married! How could he when he was already married?* Barbra felt faint.

Grace became very concerned seeing the distress on Barbra's face. Grace hurried to a side table and poured sherry into a cut crystal glass. Handing the glass to Barbra she said, thinking Barbra was hurt for not being invited to the wedding, "It was a very small and private wedding. I am sure if the Count knew you were in Gary, you would have been invited." When Barbra said nothing, Grace went on, "Are you a sister, a cousin."

Barbra went pale. It was as if she had been hit in the stomach. She wanted to lie down on the settee and curl her body into a ball.

Grace was frightened. She didn't know this woman and she didn't want to deal with a sick woman she had never met before. She ran quickly pulling open the door and calling out to Bobo, "Driver, driver, come quickly."

By the tone of Grace's voice, Bobo knew something was not right. He hurried almost running into the house, where he saw a pale almost faint Barbra on the settee.

Protective of Barbra, Bobo demanded of the white woman, "What did you do to Miss Barbra?"

A very concerned Grace Adams said, "I didn't do anything. We were just talking. Get her out of here. She is a stranger to me."

Bobo helped a weak Barbra to her feet. Bobo held her up as they walked out the door to the buggy, gently helping her onto the seat.

Grace Adams came running out of the house with the bolt of fabric. She pushed the material on Barbra's lap, not asking for or waiting for payment. Without a word she hurried back into her house.

"Miss Barbra, what did that woman do to you?" asked Bobo, giving his horse a flick of the reins to hurry the animal.

Barbra said nothing her mind full of thoughts. *Why did she care about Stefan? Why did the news that he married again affect her so? Did she still love him, even when she swore to herself that she never wanted to see him?*

Bobo looked at Barbra asking, "Are you going to be alright? We will be home soon. Just you don't faint or get sick."

Once through the gate, at the kitchen door, Bobo called out, "Ignatz, somebody, come help me!"

Ignatz was through the door immediately, followed by Josef, who could tell by look on Barbra's face that something was wrong.

Josef took Barbra in his arms. Her hat fell to the ground as he carried her into the kitchen. He tried to settle her in a chair, but she clung onto him, her arms around his neck. He backed himself into a chair, holding Barbra as one would hold a child. He felt her warm tears on his neck.

Bobo was at the kitchen door holding the bolt of fabric. Seeing him, Josef asked, "What happened?"

"I don't know." said Bobo. "The lady Barbra went to see came running out of the house, calling me. I found Barbra pale like she was going to faint. I helped her into the buggy and got here as fast as I could."

Bobo placed the bolt of rose fabric on the table. He stood around waiting to see if he was needed. After a few moments, he quietly went back to the yard.

Ignatz, not taking the time to find the proper glass, poured some kruškovac, Barbra's favorite pear brandy, into a cup.

He handed the cup to Josef, who with concerned eyes, looked at Barbra, saying softly, "Come now, Barbra. Sit up and take a sip. This will make you feel better."

Barbra would not let go of her grip on Josef. She held her hands tightly around his neck. He was all she had. She wasn't going to let him go. She couldn't bear to be alone in this foreign place.

Stevo was at the store entrance finishing up with the lamp salesman, Jim Slade. Jim, for a while, sold Katya's and Cleona's Royal products. He had even taken Katya to a Gypsy camp near Whiting.

Stevo saw Jim Slade look around the store as if wanting to find someone. He was a handsome man, always well dressed and always driving a fancy automobile

"What are you looking for?" asked Stevo.

Jim, with a sheepish grim said, "Well, Steve, I was hoping to see your new saleslady. I saw her yesterday when you were away." With a sigh he asked, "Where do you find such beautiful women?"

With a friendly shove, Stevo pushed Jim Slade out the door. "Never mind, Barbra is too much for you."

Jim tried to look back into the store, one more time, hoping to see Barbra.

He said, "Well, I will be back. I think I will deliver the lamps myself instead of having the order shipped."

Stevo smiled to himself waiving a final goodbye to the salesman as he closed the door.

Picking up his copy of the lamp order, Stevo headed for his desk near the kitchen door. Through the closed door, he could hear Josef's voice. The tone of his voice and other sounds caused Stevo to open the door.

To his surprise, he saw Barbra in Josef's lap, his arms around her, trying to console her.

Stevo stepped into the kitchen. He saw a concerned Ignatz standing in front of Barbra holding the cup of brandy. Seeing Stevo, Ignatz only shrugged his shoulders, indicating he didn't know what was wrong with Barbra.

Stevo pulled up a chair alongside Josef and Barbra. He tried to take one of Barbra's hands, but she clung to Josef's neck.

"Barbra," said Stevo, in a soothing voice, "please tell us what is wrong."

When she didn't respond, Stevo said in a very firm, but not angry voice, "Stop it, Barbra! Tell us what is wrong."

Stevo's command reached Barbra. Still holding onto Josef, her sobbing slowed. Josef felt her hold around his neck lessening. He pulled her hands away.

She straightened up, still sitting on Josef's lap, her eyes red with crying and her face wet from tears.

Stevo reached into his pocket handing Barbra a clean handkerchief.

She dabbed her eyes, wiped her face, and blew her nose.

Ignatz pulled another chair which he placed between Josef and Stevo. Stevo reached for Barbra's hand, while Josef gently lifted her from his lap. The two men settled her in the chair.

Barbra looked at the three men, not knowing what to say, feeling somewhat embarrassed. Ignatz offered the cup of brandy, he still held for her.

She sipped the brandy with downcast eyes. Barbra had never lost control of herself before. Not when her father died, not when she found the store in Zagreb closed and Stefan gone. Not even when she saw Stefan at the Gary Hotel with the American woman.

It seemed a very long moment when Barbra handed the empty cup to Ignatz. She took a deep breath straightened herself in the chair and blew her nose once again.

Her voice was low and small as she said, "Stefan got married." She saw the looks of surprise on the three men's faces. She continued, "The woman who I went to see for the fabric told me Count Vladeslav got married, when she heard my name."

Instantly, Stevo knew it had been Grace Adams Barbra went to see. Grace was a close friend of Adele Manning, the woman Stefan was seen with at the Gary Hotel.

Stevo asked, "Why are you so upset? Not long ago you said you wanted to kill Stefan. I think you even said you didn't care if you ever saw him again."

Barbra looked from Stevo to Josef.

"Don't you see? I wanted to hurt him. I wanted to show him that he meant nothing to me. Instead, I am the one hurt, abandoned.

Stevo said, "Don't think that way. You have the three of us. We will never leave you.

Barbra reached out taking Josef's hand. "Oh, Josef!" she said, "You are all I have left. Please, please never leave me. What would I do without you?"

Stevo felt something deep inside of him, he hadn't expected. It was as though he and Ignatz were not in the room. He saw the look on Barbra's face and the loving look in Josef's eyes. It was obvious he and Ignatz were in the way.

Without a word to Ignatz, Stevo indicated with a tilt of his head that they both go out in the yard. Once outside, Stevo took a deep breath. He didn't think he would ever feel anything for another woman after his Katya. Stevo felt a little guilt and shame for having allowed himself for what he was beginning to feel for Barbra.

Stevo offered Ignatz a cigarette, before lighting one for himself. Ignatz thanked him with a nod as he went to the barn to look for the dog, Mali.

Stevo sat at the table. He looked out at the swirling dust in the yard, watched some birds chasing one another in the air, heard children on the street running and laughing.

He was feeling very much alone.

CHAPTER 12

After dropping off the rose-patterned fabric sample with Barbra, Cleona walked to Milan's tavern to teach Ivanka how to use the pedal sewing machine. Something the girl had never seen before.

Cleona hadn't walked this way in a while and was surprised to see a house being built where once there were trees and the romping goats she now owned.

She knocked at the back door of the tavern, which led to the living quarters. After a while, Milan answered her knock.

"Cleona," he said, pleasantly surprised, "what brings you here?"

"I be looking for Ivanka. I'm gonna teach her to use the sewing machine."

"Sewing machine?" Milan looked confused. "When did she get a sewing machine?"

"Mato bought a sewing machine yesterday at Mr. Steve's." explained Cleona. "He bought the best one."

Milan smiled. *Of course Mato would buy Ivanka a sewing machine*, he thought to himself. *He is secretly crazy about the girl*.

"Ivanka is in the house." He pointed to the unfinished building behind Cleona. "I better get Mato to help. Ivanka doesn't speak enough English to understand you."

In less than a minute, a smiling Mato joined Cleona. He led her to the side door used by Ivanka, which led to the room where she slept.

Mato knocked softly on the door before opening it to reveal Ivanka sitting on a very narrow sleeping cot. She had been sitting there staring at the beautiful piece of furniture in the middle of the room, which hid the sewing machine.

Ivanka's heart sank when she saw Cleona. She was afraid to reveal to the little black woman and to Mato how dumb she was. Ivanka just knew she would never learn to use that thing.

Cleona was taken aback for just a moment, when she recognized the green blouse and skirt Ivanka wore. Those had been Katya's favorites.

"Come on, Ivanka." said Mato, taking her by the hand, "Time for sewing school."

A very nervous Ivanka stood in front of the lovely piece of furniture. She watched as Cleona opened the door, lifted the lid and pulled out the sewing head, anchoring it in place.

From the corner of the room, Mato fetched a straight-backed wooden chair, placing it in front of the sewing machine. "Sit here." he said to Ivanka.

Not only was the girl afraid of the machine, but she was afraid of how little she knew. She had never seen a sewing machine before visiting Stevo's store.

Ivanka was so nervous she barely understood the feeding of thread on the bobbin. The threading of the machine was confusing, a maze of holes to put the thread into and then down into the tiny hole in the needle.

Cleona sensed that Ivanka was very uncomfortable with Mato watching. It was obvious the girl was afraid of disappointing him.

"Mato," said Cleona, "you go back to work. Ivanka and I will get along just fine."

When he started to protest, Cleona said. "I don't need to speak your language to show her how to sew. You go. If I need you, I will call."

So it began. Cleona pointed to each place on the machine, where Ivanka had to insert the thread. Over and over, Cleona would point. At last Cleona put her hands on her hips pointed to the machine and then pointed to Ivanka. Ivanka, with some degree of confidence, understood that she was to thread the machine alone.

When she completed the task perfectly, her face beamed with joy and pride.

Ivanka was a bit startled when Cleona bent down and placed the girl's feet on the iron pedal. Cleona pushed down on one knee and then the other, showing Ivanka that when she did that, the needle went up and down.

From her bag, Cleona pulled out a long piece of narrow cloth. She raised her finger for Ivanka to watch. Placing the cloth under the needle and releasing the presser foot to hold the fabric, Cleona indicated for Ivanka to pedal. At first she pedaled too fast, but after a while she got into the rhythm and her face glowed with pleasure when she saw what she was doing. She was sewing! She couldn't believe it. She was sewing and it wasn't as hard as she thought. Ivanka was so excited that when she finished sewing on the piece of cloth, she cut the thread with scissors Cleona gave her and started sewing on the same piece of cloth again.

Cleona stood behind the girl, smiling. She was pleased seeing the girl happily sewing.

Ivanka was filled with a new confidence. Confidence she didn't have before. If she could learn to master this machine, what else could she learn?

Cleona pulled out more pieces of cloth for Ivanka to practice with. She placed them on the side of the machine and touched the girl's shoulder. Cleona motioned that she had to leave.

Ivanka in a burst of gratitude rose from her chair and threw her arms around Cleona. Cleona did more than teach her how to sew, but showed Ivanka she had the ability to learn new things.

Cleona slipped into the back door of the tavern, into the living quarters, she waived goodbye to Milan, not seeing Mato.

Milan came to the door. "How is she doing?" he asked.

"Just fine. She is sewing up a storm on some cloth I left with her." said Cleona. "I best be goin."

As she walked away, Milan called after her, "How are the goats?" referring to the goats he gave her when his wife Roza left.

"Doin fine, now we got three. Maybe we get another baby this year."

After a while, Ivanka stopped sewing and stared pleasingly at the pieces of cloth with stitching on them. She had done it!

Back home in Strašnik, her father and brother treated her as if she were a dumb woman, good enough only to cook, wash clothes and feed the animals. *Well*, thought Ivanka, *I am not so dumb. I came to America alone, am working for Milan and Mato, and now I learned how to use a sewing machine!*

She stood staring at the machine. It was more than a thing to sew with. It was to her a symbol, a symbol that she could learn so much more. She wanted to learn to read and after that she wanted to learn to write!

Ivanka did not close the cabinet, she left it open in the middle of the room almost as a trophy to her new confidence. She knew she had to go to work in the tavern. As soon as she could come back, she would practice sewing again. Her mind was full of things she wanted to make, not only the curtains, but clothes for herself.

Mato and Milan both noticed something different about Ivanka when she came into the tavern. *Did her face glow*? Wondered Mato. She looked so happy, smiling and nodding to the men around the bar. She gave Mato a big smile as she picked up a tray to gather used glasses from the tables.

"How did it go?" asked Mato.

"I can sew!" she said with pride. Walking away from the bar she said, "I'm not so dumb."

Milan overheard the remark. He asked his brother, "Did you tell her she was dumb?"

Wondering about the remark, Mato shook his head no.

Ivanka was happy as she worked in the bar. Her good mood and smiling face lifted the spirits of the tired worn out mill workers after their long shifts. Many of the regular customers were aware of the change in her. She had always been polite and pleasant, but never in such a happy mood as she was today.

The bar always seemed to be full of men, never giving Ivanka a chance to slip away and practice her sewing. It was about nine o'clock in the evening when Milan gave her the nod that she could leave.

She practically ran out the door to her room. There it waited for her, the beautiful machine that proved to Ivanka she could learn new things.

Ivanka sewed until the bobbin went empty. When the stitching failed, she stared at the machine. She lifted the presser foot, and looked into the space below it, seeing the empty bobbin she thought to herself, *I can do this.*

And she did! She then continued to sew over the pieces of already sewn material. She needed more cloth.

Mato also slept in the unfinished house. He used a different entrance at the front of the house. Seeing the light in her room, he knocked gently at the inner door across the hall from where he slept.

"Ivanka? Are you alright?" he asked through the closed door.

The door swung open, with Ivanka holding up pieces of cloth with stitching and threads streaming from them.

"Look, Mato. See, I can sew!" She held the pieces of cloth up to his face for him to see her accomplishments.

She was as happy as a child with a new toy. Mato could only smile at her joy, saying, "I knew you could do it." He took one of the cloths in his hands and looked at the stitching. "You sew so well. I can see how even the stitching is." He handed the cloth back to Ivanka. "Tomorrow we will go and buy some material for you to make your curtains. And…and maybe you can find come cloth to make something for yourself."

Ivanka was speechless. She stared at this wonderful man.

When she said nothing, Mato became embarrassed. He said, "Well, lako noch, good night."

Ivanka watched as he went to his room and closed the door. She stared at the closed door for a few moments. On a side table was her kerosene lantern. She turned out the light.

Ivanka walked across the short way to Mato's door. She knocked softly.

Opening the door, naked to his waist, he was surprised to see Ivanka standing there. She had never crossed the hall before.

"What's the matter?" he asked.

Ivanka entered the room, closing the door behind her.

"Ivanka, do you know what you are doing? Do you know what this means?"

Mato liked Ivanka too much to ruin the friendship they already had.

Mastering the Minnesota sewing machine had filled Ivanka with confidence. Confidence, neither she, nor Mato had expected.

CHAPTER 13

The following morning, Mato and Ivanka entered the tavern together smiling. Leaving to get a towel with which to clean the tables, Ivanka gave Mato a special knowing smile, which did not escape Milan.

Milan watched his younger brother grin as he came behind the bar.

"I'll be damned." said Milan. "You got her!"

Mato's grin turned into a large smile. "No, she got me."

Milan stared at his brother then looked out into the room at Ivanka gathering used glasses.

"So, she got you." he said pleased, "I'll be damned."

The room had only a few men coming off the night shift, looking for a place to sit and have a beer before going to the rooming houses they lived in, usually where they shared a bed with another mill worker.

Milan opened the entry door, bracing it open with a large stone. The smoke filled room needed airing. He walked around the room, opening the windows before turning on the standing fan to blow out the stale air.

At a far table two men, still in their soiled work clothes, starting cursing and shouting at one another. As one man rose, his chair fell over and he grabbed at the still seated man by the collar.

Milan was used to these fights. He headed across the room to break it up. He usually either grabbed the fighters and threw them out, or if able, calmed them down and gave them a free beer.

When he neared the table he saw that one of the men had a knife.

"Hey!" he shouted. "Not in here. No knife fighting!"

Milan tried to get in between the men to stop the fight. A flying fist found Milan's face. Milan was taken by surprise. Usually when he went to break up a fight, the men calmed down, knowing Milan could and would throw them out.

The pain Milan felt in his stomach was something he had never felt before. The two fighters backed away as Milan grabbed at the table top for support, before he sank to the floor.

Both men ran to the door, knocking a stunned Mato aside. The few morning patrons stared in shock, too stunned or frightened to try and stop the fleeing men.

Ivanka screamed, running to the fallen Milan. With the cleaning towel in her hand, she pressed it to his bleeding wound. She lifted his head on her lap, tears streaming down her cheeks.

Sensing the seriousness of Milan's wound, the few patrons headed for the exit. Only one older bearded man with longish hair stayed at the bar.

Mato ran to his brother. He was shaking with fear and shock seeing his brother pale and visibly getting weaker.

"Call a doctor! Get a doctor!" shouted Ivanka, pressing hard on Milan's wound.

Mato, in shock, didn't grasp her words, until she hit him on the shoulder bringing him out of his daze. "Get a doctor!" she shouted again.

Mato stumbled to the bar, where behind it was a telephone in a box, deliberately hidden from the patrons, who just might make calls if they knew it was available.

For a moment, Mato's brain was blank. He couldn't remember Stevo's phone number. Then it came to him, 22. He dialed the number and Tomo answered. He had a hard time understanding his hysterical friend, but when he did understand, Tomo shouted, "We are coming!"

From the kitchen table, Stevo and Josef heard Tomo's panicked voice. Both men stood as Tomo came running into the room shouting, "Milan's been stabbed."

With his instinct as a doctor, Josef ran up the stairs with the speed of a marathon runner. He grabbed his medical satchel and descended the steps in giant leaps, missing several steps as he flew down.

Bobo had already prepared the horse and buggy wanting to take Barbra for an outing, hoping the fresh air and ride would help her get over yesterday's shock at hearing Stefan had married.

The three men squeezed into the buggy, surprising Bobo, who was expecting only Barbra.

"Come on, Bobo! Get moving, Milan's been hurt." shouted Stevo.

Bobo whipped the horse and the men arrived quickly, as the tavern was within walking distance.

Josef was the first out of the buggy. He ran through the open door, immediately seeing Ivanka on the floor with Milan. Mato was on his knees, his hands folded rocking back and forth repeating, "Sveti Isus…Holy Jesus and Maika Boze…Blessed Mother."

Stevo ran to see Milan, while Tomo closed the door, latching it so that no customers could come in.

Turning from the door, Tomo noticed the one man at the bar.

Tomo said, "When you finish your drink, perhaps you should leave."

The man said, "I was only staying to tell someone what I heard one of the men say as they ran out."

"What was that?" asked Tomo.

"All I heard was 'that was for Roza'."

Tomo sank onto the bar stool next to the man. Not again, thought Tomo, remembering the night he was so badly beaten by men from Whiting who came looking to beat up Milan. Men sent by Roza to avenge her because Milan threw her out of the tavern and his life.

Milan wasn't there that night almost a year ago. Roza had been insanely jealous of Katya, so when the men heard that Tomo was close to Katya, they gave him the beating meant for Milan.

Sick to his stomach, Tomo asked the man, "Would you like another beer?"

"No, he said, "I just stayed to tell someone what I heard. I don't need to be here." He glanced back at the cluster of people around Milan on the floor. "Only family should be here now."

The man got up from the bar stool, feeling the aches of working a 14-hour shift at the mill. He touched his cap with his fingers as a goodbye gesture and went out the door.

A couple men tried to enter, but Tomo stopped them with, "We are closed today. Sorry, we are closed." He went to the door and locked it again.

Stevo felt weak. He sat on a chair at the table next to the fallen Milan. He looked down at his friend and felt as if he was going to be sick. Sarcastic, ornery, full of mischief and the devil, Milan now lay on the floor, his face with no color. He was a pale white.

With Josef attending to Milan, Ivanka, sitting on the floor, leaned against the wall, her legs stretched out before her. She had stopped crying. Now she felt numb, fearing the worst. Milan was like a brother to her. He had treated her better than her own brother had back in Strašnik.

Now was no time for Ivanka to faint or get sick. She heard Mato cry out, "Ah yoy, ah yoy..." holding his head as he rocked back and forth kneeling next to his brother. She knelt beside Mato wrapping her arms around him.

Josef looked up at Stevo, with sadness, shaking his head, indicating that Milan was gone.

For the second time in a little less than a year, Stevo felt a numbing loss. *Not again,* he thought. The two people who meant the most to him were gone, first his beloved, Katya, and now his dear friend, Milan.

Ivanka helped Mato to a chair at the table near where Stevo was seated. Mato dropped his head on the table and sobbed. Stevo was too numb to cry.

Josef motioned to Tomo for assistance. The two men pushed together two square tables, where they lifted and placed Milan' body.

Josef, his shirt sleeves stained with Milan's blood, placed a hand on Stevo's shoulder. "Come," he said, "come to the bar with me."

Ivanka took Tomo, just as heartsick as the others, by the elbow. She said, "Tomo, please write a sign for the door. Something like, "Closed due to death in family."

Tomo went behind the bar looking for some cardboard to write on. Josef was behind the bar looking for some brandy. Tomo motioned to the bottle saying, "Pour one for me."

Ready with a hammer and nails, Ivanka took the sign from Tomo, going out to place it on the door.

The room was quiet, except for the moans and sobs of Mato. Ivanka went to him with a glass of slivovitz in her hand. She placed it before him.

"Here. Drink this." she said. She stood waiting for him to finish his drink. Back in the kitchen, she got a clean towel and wet it in cool water. She wrung it out and took it to Mato, who immediately placed in on his face and held it there.

Ivanka went back to the bar. She studied the three sad men. No one was speaking, each lost in their own thoughts, especially, Josef, the doctor. This was his first call in America and he didn't save his patient.

Tomo was standing behind the bar while Josef and Stevo sat on bar stools.

Ivanka went to stand beside Tomo. She asked, "How do you prepare and bury people here in America? If I were home in Strašnik women would come help me prepare the body."

None of the men spoke, they just looked at her.

She continued, "Then the neighbor men would build a coffin and dig the grave."

Stevo cleared his throat before saying, "Ivanka, we, Tomo, Marjan, and I will take care of everything."

Seeing the confused look on Ivanka's face, Stevo continued, "You see, Ivanka, we not only sell furniture, but we conduct funerals as well."

Mato approached his group of friends, the damp towel now draped around his neck. Still a little pale, eyes reddened from crying, he said, "We will close the tavern for three days, maybe more. We will have the visitation and prayers here."

The words caught in his throat. He waited a moment, composing himself then continued. "After the funeral, we will have the karmina…funeral luncheon here."

Ivanka was behind Mato. She put her arms around him, leaning her head against his back.

Everyone was silent for a while.

Finally, Stevo said, "Tomo, Marjan and I will be back in a little while to prepare Milan." He couldn't say 'the body'. "Get some clean clothes and his suit. For now you two go in back and rest. We will take care of everything."

No one called the police for this was The Patch where the immigrants took care of their own.

CHAPTER 14

When Stevo and Tomo returned that evening with a casket to prepare Milan's body, Stevo brought the black dress Katya had worn to her first husband's funeral for Ivanka, who was so very pleased to receive it.

Ivanka and Mato stayed in the living quarters at the back of the tavern, too emotional to watch Stevo and Milan as they worked.

As instructed, clean clothes were laid out on a nearby table.

Tomo and Stevo, so filled with emotion at the loss of their friend, barely spoke as the worked.

Stevo's mind was filled with so many memories of his and Milan's friendly rivalry for Katya's affection.

Tomo noticed Stevo brush a tear from his cheek.

Milan was placed in one of the nicer caskets, one that the mill workers could never have afforded.

Mato, his face looking pale and ill, came from the living quarters. He swayed slightly when he saw his older brother, so nicely dressed in the brass-trimmed oak coffin. In Mato's hand were two bottles, the bottles that Mato had seen his brother handle often, Katya's Royal Witch Hazel and Royal Honey Cream.

"Put these in with him." said Mato.

Tomo placed the bottles out of sight, between Milan's arm and the satin lining of the casket.

Stevo said, "I'll contact the priest for the church burial."

"No, don't do that." said Mato. "Milan would not want to be in a church."

A bit surprised, Stevo said, "What are you talking about? Milan made one of the largest donations for the Holy Trinity Church fund."

Mato went to a nearby table and sat. "I know." he said. "But he held a personal grudge against the church from something that happened back home in our village."

Seeing the look of interest on Tomo and Stevo's faces, Mato continued, "A big storm was coming, so our father harvested the crop on a Sunday to try and save what he could. The local priest heard of this and our father was sent to prison, leaving Milan and me, just young boys, to take care of the farm until he returned."

Stevo nodded. He could understand Milan's grudge. Stevo had seen how hard Milan could be when he felt cheated or crossed in some way.

"I'll see what I can do." Stevo said.

Word spread quickly within the Croatian community. Many people were saddened by Milan's death. Even those who did not visit the tavern knew of his generosity, though he had never spoken of it. There were times he saw to it that a widow had food for her children, or when he made a loan, it was often a gift for he never demanded it be paid back.

The next morning, nearly everyone knew that the visitation for Milan was to be held at the tavern in the evening.

Bobo and Marjan borrowed chairs from any business that could spare them for two days, in anticipation of a large crowd.

Barbra and Josef walked to the tavern, in the hopes they could help.

On the closed door of the tavern was a sign:

Visitation tonight, 6 to 8.

Funeral tomorrow, 10 o'clock.

Ivanka was pleased to see Barbra. She hugged her new friend and took her to the living quarters in the back, while Josef helped place the borrowed chairs around the room.

Barbra looked around the space where Mato and Milan had lived before the building of the new house. It was nice, considering it did not have a feminine touch anywhere. One entered the kitchen from the tavern where next there was a small room with some comfortable seating. Then there were two small bedrooms. The arrangement was long and narrow, but adequate. Enough so, that Ivanka liked it and could envision how much nicer it could be.

When the chairs were all in place, there wasn't much more for the men to do.

Mato said, "Let's have drink to my brother."

Josef, who didn't know Milan very well, was touched by the affection Stevo and Tomo had for the big man. Josef hoped that he would be liked, loved as Milan was.

Mato poured slivovitz, the plum brandy, into glasses for all of them.

Tomo raised his glass, "To Milan, our friend." he said.

Their glasses empty, the men refused a second drink. There were more arrangements to be made. Marjan had been sent to the cemetery with instructions for the burial, while Bobo was on his way to arrange for men to come before daylight to prepare the lambs for roasting in the yard behind the tavern for the karmina, the memorial luncheon.

Ivanka came into the tavern with Barbra at her side. She asked, "Can a couple of you men bring my sewing machine into the rooms in back?"

Mato looked surprised.

Ivanka said, "Mato and I will live here, in back."

Even through his heartbreak, Mato showed a small pleased smile."

Barbra followed the men out the door to the nearly finished house. They all entered the side door to Ivanka's room.

Tomo closed the machine, so it was now looking like a side cabinet. He and Mato easily lifted and carried it, following Ivanka who knew where she wanted it placed. Stevo walked with them.

Barbra and Josef were alone in the small room Ivanka had slept in.

Barbra said, "Can we go look around?"

"I suppose so." said, Josef, taking her hand. "I don't think anyone lives here."

The house was almost completed. It was a long narrow house with a pitched roof. It needed some painting and the installation of electricity had yet to be completed.

Josef, in his shirt sleeves and Barbra, holding up her long blue skirt, went outside through the side door. They went to the front door and found it unlocked.

The entrance was a small hallway, with a door to the right and one to the left. These were the rooms Mato and Ivanka used. As Barbra and Josef walked further into the hallway, they saw an unfinished kitchen, a parlor and two more small rooms, possibly bedrooms.

Josef and Barbra did not go up to the second floor, which from where they stood, looked like an attic.

Barbra said, "This could be made into a very nice place to live."

Josef said nothing. He was thinking the two rooms at the entrance would be a waiting room for patients and the other his treatment room.

At six o'clock, the tavern started to fill with friends to offer their condolences and mourn the loss of a man who had quietly been valuable to the community.

Stevo managed to talk the priest from Holy Trinity into coming to say the Rosary. It wasn't easy, since Stevo had to tell him that there would be no burial Mass. It took more persuading to get the priest to agree to come to the cemetery to conduct a service there.

Marjan stood behind the bar lined with glasses. He offered a drink to anyone who wanted one. The men were all polite, taking only one drink in honor of Milan.

During the Rosary, almost everyone knelt on the freshly-mopped floor.

Like a mantra, the Rosary was said, Sveta Mayka Boze…Hail Mary, mother of God, and so it went.

Stevo was not kneeling. He sat alone in a far corner of the room watching the people pray and the priest kneeling before the coffin.

Something since Milan's death disturbed Stevo greatly. He felt a loneliness that even Katya's death did not create. Milan had been Stevo's connection to Katya, a connection to fun and loving times.

Stevo looked around the room at all the familiar faces. People he thought of as friends. He looked across the room to Marjan at the bar, at Tomo near the casket alongside Mato and Ivanka. Near the wall was Ignatz, also on his knees. Barbra and Josef were close to Ignatz.

In a room with all these people Stevo knew, shared happy and sad times with, ate and drank with, he felt a profound loneliness. As if he no longer belonged here.

CHAPTER 15

The day of the funeral saw the tavern crowded with mourners.

The women, who had no black dresses, wore back aprons over their full skirts and black crocheted shawls around their shoulders. Almost all the men wore a black arm band on their sleeve.

After the prayer by the priest, people passed by the casket for a last look at Milan. Many paused to take a long look. Some touched his hand in a farewell.

Outside the tavern waited the buggy driven by Bobo with Ignatz at his side. This buggy was used as a hearse. Behind it was a two seat carriage where the priest and Tomo sat in the front with Mato and Ivanka in the rear seat. The last carriage was driven by Stevo with Cleona at his side. Behind them sat Barbra and Josef.

Several men acting as pall bearers carried out the casket and placed it the buggy where Bobo waited.

Behind the last carriage, the musicians, the tamburashi, walked, playing the music they all loved from back home in Croatia.

A trail of scattered groups of people followed the musicians on foot to the Tolleston Cemetery.

The pall bearers placed the casket on the straps, while the priest stood nearby waiting. The people crowded around the grave.

Cleona, standing next to Stevo, grabbed his arms, tears in her eyes. The words caught in her throat as she said, "Oh, Mister Steve, you done give him to Katya."

Milan's grave was alongside Katya's. This spot was usually reserved for the spouse.

Tomo was the only other person who realized that Milan was placed beside Katya. He looked from the other side of the grave and smiled at Stevo, nodding his approval.

There was crying as the casket was lowered. Even Barbra, who hardly knew Milan, cried. Perhaps she was crying for her father, or for Stefan, or just for the fact that her future was so uncertain.

Mato went to the casket and placed both hands on it, his final farewell to his brother.

Mourners with flowers in their hands, some purchased, some from their own gardens, placed them on the casket before it was lowered.

Stevo, with Cleona at his side, stepped in front of the grave. He announced, "Mato and Ivanka would be pleased if all of you would come back to the tavern for the karmina. I think you all smelled the yanyetina…lamb roasting in back of the tavern.

That announcement ended the funeral so the carriages went directly to the tavern. There were details to take care of before the people arrived to eat.

Scattered groups of friends walked back to the tavern, no longer in a procession.

Back at the tavern, the carriages and horses were driven to the far side of the new house, in a shaded, grassy area.

Bobo and Ignatz went to where the meat was being roasted. It smelled wonderful.

Inside, Mato went to a table and sat. He was feeling terribly sad. Ivanka patted his shoulder, gave him a kiss on the cheek, saying, "You just sit here. We will take care of everything.

While the funeral was taking place, Stevo arranged for women to come in and line up the tables in long rows. Baskets of bread were on the tables, along with trays of peeled green onions. A glass was at each place along with cloth napkins. No knives or forks were needed for the roasted lamb.

Before finding a chair, a very old woman went out to the yard. She asked Ignatz, "Will you give me the head?"

Behind Ignatz, a man in a no longer clean apron, was chopping the cooked lamb into pieces to place on plates.

Ignatz pointed to the butcher saying, "As soon as he finishes, I will bring in the head. Watch for me."

The wrinkled old Baba, all in black, smiled at Ignatz, showing a missing front tooth.

In a matter of minutes, Ignatz and Bobo entered carrying plates of chopped lamb to the tables.

Seeing Ignatz, the old woman stood up and waived to him. He delivered the plate with the lamb's head to her. She loved eating the roasted eyes.

The mood of the people was shifting from mournful to slightly happy. The tamburashi were playing livelier music and the conversations in the room and sound levels were rising.

Barbra carried pitchers of beer to the tables and it made her feel like the girl she was back in her Uncle Fritz's tavern in Germany. People smiled at her and made her feel part of the Croatian community.

The front doors opened and men came in holding huge trays of strudels, frosted cakes, and cookies.

Seeing all the food and the preparation, and now all the platters of sweets, Mato, with a pang of guilt, wondered how he was going to pay for all this. He was still wondering about the cost of the elegant casket.

Cleona found smaller plates on which she made up an assortment of the baked goods. She walked among the tables, placing the plates here and there.

Everyone seemed to be enjoying Milan's last party. The people would talk about this for a long time.

Barbra carried a pitcher of beer out to the men who cooked the lambs. They were sitting on tree stumps and boxes, enjoying what they do and the company of the men they were with.

Cleona was close behind Barbra with a dish piled high with the bakery goods.

Stories about Milan were told, cigarettes were lit, singing was heard, and toasts to Milan were offered again and again.

Even Mato was starting to relax and not feel so terribly sad.

Everyone was enjoying the food, the company, and the atmosphere. That is all except Stevo. He sat in the same spot he had the night before, in the far corner of the room, alone. He sipped his glass of beer, but didn't eat any food.

No one knew it yet, but Stevo was paying for all the food and the hired help.

A young, pretty girl in braids was behind the bar with Marjan. Stevo had no idea who she was. He had no idea that Marjan had invited the Slovak girl, Mara, the one he was smitten with, to the tavern.

Ignatz brought plates to the bar for Marjan and Mara. The girl was so impressed with all the food. She wished she could take some home to her poor family.

Josef sat with people he had never met. Several people had heard he was a ljechnik, a doctor. They were asking him so many questions. Did he have an office? Could they come to him? Would he come out to the house? Could he wait for his fee to be paid?

Josef, his handsome face relaxed, smiled at the attention he was getting. For the first time since coming to America, he was feeling like his real self.

As the luncheon wound down and people were leaving, some of them dropped coins or bills into a basket which had been placed on the bar. It was not necessary to drop money in the basket, still some did.

Some hours later, when most of the people were gone, Ivanka, Mato, Barbra, Ignatz, Tomo, Josef, and Cleona sat at a table. Enough time to clean up tomorrow.

Marjan left to walk Mara home. He did manage to take a plate of cakes to give to her family.

Cleona took a sip of slivovitz. Squinting her eyes she made a face and shook her head. "How come you people ain't dead from drinking this stuff?"

Everyone laughed at her.

Cleona looked around. "Where is Mister Steve?" she asked.

Josef said, "As a matter of fact, I haven't seen him most of the afternoon. I just thought he was mingling. Maybe he is outside."

Cleona stood up. "I guess I better be leavin." To Mato, she said, "You want me to come help clean up tomorrow?"

Mato stood, taking Cleona's hand. "No thank you, Cleona. We will be closed tomorrow plenty of time for us to clean." he said.

Once outside, Cleona walked as fast as she could. She knew Mister Steve wasn't himself ever since Milan was killed.

When she got to the back gate of the store yard, she pushed it open then closed it again.

The kitchen door was unlocked. She entered. It was very quiet. She looked into the store and saw that the shades had been drawn to indicate it was closed.

She stood still and listened. Hearing nothing, she went to the stairs. Again she listened.

Without making a sound, she ascended the stairs. She didn't feel right. It was too quiet. At the top of the stairs, Cleona walked past each room, not seeing Stevo in any of them.

At the end of the hall was the chapel Stevo had built as a surprise for Katya. She so often spoke of the chapel behind the Vladeslav house and how much she loved it, so he had this one made especially for her.

Cleona looked into the tiny room. Stevo was seated on the bench in front of the tiny altar. He never used the kneeler, only the bench.

Concerned, Cleona asked, "You alright, Mister Steve?"

When he didn't reply, she asked, "What you doin here?"

With the saddest look Cleona had ever seen on a person's face, Stevo said, "I'm thinking."

CHAPTER 16

Some two weeks passed since the funeral of Milan. Those close to Stevo were aware of the change in him. He was very quiet, seemingly lost in thought.

Tomo was quite disturbed seeing that Stevo no longer had any interest in the management of the store. Decisions that Stevo once made, now fell to Tomo. The first few times Tomo had to make an important decision, he didn't think very much of it, but when he found himself just about completely in charge, he became quite worried.

Tomo insisted his brother work harder at learning to speak English. Marjan was now so in love with the Slovak girl, Mara, that he spent nearly every evening visiting the girl and taking her for long walks. Sometimes they would take a streetcar ride into downtown Gary, again just walking and looking into the shop windows.

Barbra and Josef helped at the store, but their thoughts were elsewhere. Both of them thought about the empty and almost completed house behind the tavern.

On several occasions during the past two weeks, they would walk to the tavern, sit at a table and talk privately about the house.

Today, Barbra said to Josef, "Should we ask Mato what his plans are about the house?" With a concerned look she said, "What if he has already sold it?"

"I've thought about that." said Josef, wiping the dampness from his hands on his handkerchief. The cold beer made the glass sweat. He put the handkerchief in his white shirt pocket. His brown jacket was draped on the back of his chair.

"We have a problem." said Josef. "We have no money with which to pay for the house and," he went on, "do we leave Stevo with no help at the store? Have you noticed the change in him? It is as if he doesn't care much about anything?"

Barbra didn't want to think about Stevo just yet. With a thoughtful look, her dark eyes serious she said, "Let's ask Mato about his plans for the house. If he will sell it to us, I think I know how we can raise the money to pay him. Then we can talk with Stevo and see how he feels about our leaving."

This remark about raising the money was a surprise to Josef. He said, "I'll see if Mato can sit with us for bit."

Waiting for Josef to return, Barbra glanced around the smoke filled room. She heard bursts of laughter here and there and an occasional swear word tossed into the air. When someone raised their glass to her in a greeting, she would waive or nod with a smile.

Mato came to the table with Josef. Smiling broadly at Barbra, Mato said, "Dobro yutro, Good morning."

Josef looked to Barbra, but she nodded that Josef should do the asking.

"Mato," began Josef, "what do you plan to do with the house in back?"

A bit surprised with the question, Mato said, "Milan and I planned to rent out the rooms, turn it into a boarding house with Ivanka as the housekeeper." He paused, still affected by the loss of his brother. Barbra and Josef waited for Mato to get control of his emotions.

Mato cleared his throat saying, "The house is finished. It is painted and the electricity is done."

Now Barbra spoke. She touched Mato's hand. "If we can raise the money would you sell the house to us?"

Mato's face registered mingled looks of surprise and pleasure.

Smiling broadly, he said, "We, Ivanka and I, would love to have you in the house." Then his look became serious, "But, what about Stevo? Doesn't he need you to help in the store?"

Josef took a sip of his beer. Putting down his glass he said, "Barbra and I have been thinking and talking about that. We don't understand the change in Stevo." Josef looked at Barbra, wondering if he was divulging too much about their new friend and host.

Barbra said, "Oh, Mato. Stevo is not the same since Milan is gone."

She saw the flicker in Mato's eyes at the mention of his brother's passing.

"I'm sorry." she said. "We wondered if you noticed the change in Stevo."

Mato said, "I haven't seen him since the funeral luncheon. I have asked Tomo when he comes here to bring me the bill, but so far he hasn't done so." Then he added, "Tomo doesn't come here as often as he used to. His brother Marjan comes almost every evening with that Mara girl."

"Back to the matter of selling the house," said Josef, "do you have any idea how much you would need for it?"

Mato saw that Ivanka was motioning that he was needed at the bar. Rising from his chair he said, "Give me some time to see what I still owe for the materials and work. I haven't thought much about it since…since the funeral."

When he was gone, Barbra said to Josef, "Let's leave. We can talk on the way back to the store. You can tell me what you think of my idea."

At the kitchen door of the store, Barbra and Josef found it empty. They walked through into the store and saw Tomo with a customer, a woman looking at oak ice boxes. Barbra led Josef to the far wall and pointed to the paintings Stefan had brought with him to America.

"Look." Barbra said, "These are by some of the finest artists in Europe, Braque and Leger. We sold some to American tourists. There must be somewhere we can sell these paintings to have money we need to buy the house."

Stevo was coming down the stairs from the living quarters above. He heard the tale end of Barbra's sentence.

Unnoticed, behind Barbra and Josef, Stevo asked, "Where is this house you want to buy?"

Surprised that Stevo overheard them, both Barbra and Josef felt guilty and it showed on their faces.

"Come into the kitchen and let's talk." said Stevo his open hand towards the kitchen door.

Once in the kitchen, the three sat down. Barbra and Josef felt as if they were betraying Stevo. Who would work the store if they were to leave? Marjan still was uncomfortable with people or with trying to show the merchandise.

Barbra looked to Josef. What could they say?

Stevo saw the look. "Come now." he said. "We are friends. Tell me what you have been thinking about. Perhaps I can help."

Josef took a deep breath. He reached for Barbra's hand saying, "We were thinking we would like to buy the house behind Mato and Ivanka. It is finished and we think it would be just right for us."

Expecting Stevo to object both Barbra and Josef were surprised to hear him ask, "Has Mato given you a price?"

Barbra was the first to speak. "We thought you might be disappointed or even angry that we wanted to leave you."

Stevo's face was melancholy. He said, "Of course you must leave if that is what you want." He paused a moment and looked at the wall instead of them. "We all must do what our hearts tell us to do."

Both Barbra and Josef were not sure what he meant. Before they could say anything Stevo asked, "Do you have the money to buy the house?"

"No." said Barbra, "Not yet."

Seeing the questioning look on Stevo's face, Josef said, "Barbra was hoping we could sell the paintings Stefan left here."

Stevo said, "I am sure they are valuable, but not for my customers."

Hearing a familiar voice, Stevo rose, going to the door that was the back entrance to the store. He saw the lamp salesman Jim Slade showing Tomo some flyers.

"Come with me." he said to Barbra and Josef.

Jim Slade, dressed as always in the most up-to-the-minute fashion, gray trousers, a checkered grey coat, white shirt, and maroon tie with black, high-top button closed shoes.

Seeing the trio walk towards him and Tomo, Jim Slade gave Barbra one of his most dazzling salesman's smiles. She smiled back at him, which encouraged him, giving him confidence that he could get to know her better.

Tomo, with the money for the sold ice box in his hand, excused himself to write down the sale and instruct Bobo to make the delivery right away.

"Sit down, Jim." said Stevo. "We would like to talk to you. Get your advice."

Jim looked a bit confused, but when he looked at Barbra's warm smile, he relaxed and sat down.

Stevo took the lead, saying, "The paintings you see on my walls belong to Barbra. They are some of her paintings from her store in Zagreb."

"I don't know, Steve." said Jim. "Why do you ask me, this isn't my usual line of merchandise?"

"We know that." said Stevo. "But, you did a good job of selling the Royal line for Katya."

Stevo looked at Jim. He could see the inner struggle taking place within the salesman. Jim looked from Stevo to Barbra and then to Josef, whom he had not been introduced to.

After a long moment Jim asked, "Are you wanting me to buy these or to find a buyer for you?" The question was directed at Barbra.

Barbra responded quickly, "Whichever way would get us the most money."

"Us?" said Jim. He looked from Barbra to Josef.

Josef spoke for the first time. He introduced himself, "I am Josef Popovich. Barbra and I knew each other in Zagreb and traveled to America together."

Stevo saw the look of disappointment on Jim's face as Josef continued, "We need money to purchase a house we like."

Stevo prompted Jim saying, "Come on Jim. You know all the fine store owners in Chicago. Surely one of them would jump at the chance to have these paintings."

Jim looked from Barbra to Josef and then to Stevo. He tapped his finger on the table, a sign that he was thinking. He let out long breath before saying, "I have an appointment with the head of the decorative designs department at Marshall Field's this afternoon."

The name Marshall Field meant nothing to Barbra or Josef, but Stevo knew it well, having taken his Katya there one happy afternoon.

Jim said, "If you can go with me now, I will introduce you to the buyer. You will have to make the sale, since I don't know anything about paintings."

"Of course we can go with you." said Barbra, reaching across the table to take Jim's hand. "You are so wonderful to do this for us."

Stevo realized that Jim needed to make something should there be a sale, so he said, "Barbra, Josef, perhaps you should discuss Jim's commission before you start taking the pictures off the wall."

Jim's face relaxed when he heard what Stevo said. It pleased him. Jim gave them a figure and when Stevo said it was fair, Barbra and Josef jumped up to remove the pictures and stacked them at the door.

While Barbra and Josef were taking down the pictures, Jim said to Stevo, "I suppose Barbra isn't coming with me alone."

"You suppose correctly." replied Stevo.

Jim Slade was driving a 1913 American Underslung automobile. It could seat four passengers, but Jim usually had boxed lamps or other merchandise on the back seat and the floor.

To make room for the paintings, Jim and Stevo carried out the few boxes of lamps from the back of the car. It took several rearrangements of the paintings to make them all fit, but not before Josef and Stevo removed the canvases from the frames.

Jim thought the removal of the frames would make selling the artwork more difficult. Once in the car, the paintings were covered with a heavy cloth, Jim always had with him.

Barbra and Josef had never ridden in an auto before, so they were excited. Barbra sat in the middle, close to Jim, which did not displease him. Her eyes were shiny with excitement and Josef, too, felt a tingle of excitement.

Barbra was hatless, but she did tie a scarf over her hair and under her chin to keep the wind from ruining her hairdo.

Josef and Jim wore hats securely on their heads not wanting to have them blow off into the road.

Barbra's eyes could not take in all the sights fast enough. She wanted to see all the buildings, the people, and especially the houses scattered not too closely on the road to Chicago.

The ride was not always smooth. There were stretches of bumpy dirt roads, some gravel roads, and not often enough, nice paved roads.

In Chicago, Barbra was in awe of the Union Stock Yards. In the distance she saw the red Exchange Buildings. Never in her life had she seen so many pens with so many cattle. All she could smell was dust and cattle. She wondered how people worked there or lived nearby with the strong cattle odor.

Because of Barbra's childlike excitement, Jim drove along the lake shore road before turning off to Michigan Avenue.

The throng of people, the cable cars, the horse drawn carriages with only a very few automobiles made Barbra's head swim. She had never seen this much activity in one street or even one city.

She saw a large sign over a building. It read C.D.PEACOCKS. She asked Jim, "They sell peacocks in that store?"

She couldn't believe him when he told her it was a high end jewelry store.

Extended from what Barbra thought were hundreds of store fronts were awnings to protect the pedestrians from the sun or rain, but mostly to protect the displayed merchandise from the damaging effect of the sun.

Jim drove the car to the back delivery entrance of Marshall Field’s. The man at the door recognized Jim.

"We need a bin for the things in the back seat." said Jim

Barbra and Josef watched as a large wicker basket on wheels was brought to the car. Two men carefully removed the protective cloth covering the paintings. The art work was carefully stacked in the large, bin-like basket.

Barbra, Josef, Jim, and one of the men in charge of the basket stepped into a freight elevator.

Barbra made a small, surprised sound when she felt the elevator start to rise.

The door opened onto a storage room for it had unopened crates and scattered excelsior on the floor used for protective packing.

A young man with a clipboard in his hand, wearing a blue, knee-length cotton coat to identify him as a stock person, upon seeing Jim Slade, said "Mr. Walters is free and can see you now." He looked questioningly at Barbra and Josef.

"We are together." said Jim, as the young man held open the door leading to the show room floor.

The displays and artifacts took Barbra's breath away. She saw a Moroccan table with intricately designed patterns of various woods. On a pedestal, she recognized a Lalique patterned vase.

Barbra and Josef were told by Jim to sit on a sofa, as an impeccably dressed man came to Jim, shaking his hand. The man wore a light brown suit with thin, darker brown lines running through the fabric. His tie was blue, with an impressive gold stickpin in it, over a blindingly white stiff-collared shirt. His highly polished shoes where not button high tops, but low with lace ties.

Barbra watched as Jim spoke with the man, who looked towards them and nodded to whatever it was that Jim was saying.

If Josef was nervous, he did not show it, but Barbra hoped her anxiety did not show. Just looking at Mr. Walters indicated to Barbra he was important.

Mr. Walters and Jim came to the sofa, Josef stood politely while Jim made the introductions.

After the introductions, Jim and Mr. Walters excused themselves and went into the store room to look at the paintings.

Mr. Walters, taking a pair of glasses from his suit pocket, put them on. He said nothing as he pulled a painting, one at a time, from wicker bin.

Jim was a bit apprehensive, for usually Mr. Walters commented on each item as he looked at it. This time he was silent, contemplative.

When he looked at the last one, he turned to Jim asking, "How is it those people have these paintings?"

"As I understand it, the lady had a store in Zagreb and brought them with her to America." said Jim.

"Do you have the power to negotiate with me?" asked Mr. Walters.

"I only promised to show the paintings to you." said Jim. "I think you should talk it over with Madam Vladeslav."

CHAPTER 17

On the ride back to Gary, Barbra could not stop talking about the beauty of the store, Marshall Field's.

Mr. Walters was so pleased with his purchase that he gave Jim, Barbra and Josef an invitation to the Walnut Room, where they had a lovely luncheon, served on white linen table cloths. Jim was impressed because in all the time he had been working with Mr. Walters, he was never offered a lunch in the Walnut Room.

After their lunch, Barbra had asked, "Do we have time to look around this beautiful store?" Jim was so pleased with the sale of the pictures and what his commission will be that he could not refuse Barbra anything.

"Sure." he said. "Let's take the elevators all the way down so you can see the main floor."

Once on the main floor, Barbra could only stare at the interior of the building. The main floor was a huge area open up to the ceiling, with each floor appearing to be on balconies. The clerks were all neatly dressed in black skirts, white blouses, with watches on chains hanging from their necks.

Surrounding this large open space, Barbra counted three levels above the main floor. She stared up at the exquisite glass ceiling, an enormous work of art by Tiffany.

Once back in Gary at Stevo's furniture store, before going up to her room, Barbra took Jim's hand saying, "Thank you, Jim. We appreciate you taking us to Chicago and arranging the sale of our paintings. It was such a wonderful day. Thank you again."

Josef also shook Jim's hand before going to the back of the store to see how Tomo was doing with sales that day.

Stevo came from the back of the store to where Jim was standing. "It looks as if you did well." said Stevo. "Have you got time to go across the street for drink?"

The two men found a small table at Strincich's liquor store. Stevo had a wine while Jim Slade had a beer.

Jim was the first to speak. "I have to thank you for talking me into taking those pictures to sell." He took a sip of beer and continued, "I am not only making a commission on the paintings, but next week I am coming with a small truck to take the frames, which incidentally is another complete sale and another commission." With a big smile he said, "This is the first time I have impressed this particular buyer."

Both men sipped their drinks without speaking for a while. Stevo was lost for a moment in the memory of the time he took Katya to Marshall Field's and purchased a beaded purse for her.

Motioning to the owner for more beer, Jim said, "That Josef doesn't talk much. He seems to be a very quiet guy."

"He's a good man." said Stevo. "In Zagreb he was a doctor and now he sells my furniture without my asking him to. I consider them both my guests, not my employees. After all, Barbra was married to Katya's cousin."

"A doctor?" Jim said surprised.

"Not everyone from Croatia is a peasant." laughed Stevo. "In fact, Barbra is a Countess."

Jim was about to say, "You're shitting me." but stopped when a man and woman walked past the table. Instead he said, "Come on Steve, you're pulling my leg. Your little gypsy Katya had a cousin who was a count?"

"True." said Stevo, "Her mother was aunt to Barbra's husband."

Before Jim could ask about Stefan, Barbra's husband, Stevo changed the topic of conversation, he wanted to get to the reason he asked Jim to come for a drink.

"Tell me, Jim" he began, "what do you think of Tom as my store manager." Stevo put up his hand before Jim could reply. "Now be honest. This is important to me."

"I think he is great." said Jim sincerely, "His English is very good and he is very polite." Jim smiled, "And, he is good looking. That is a plus in business."

Stevo finished his wine. Jim motioned to the waiter, pointing to Stevo's glass for a refill.

Jim said, "Why do you ask?"

"Do you think he could run the store if I were to take a trip?" asked Stevo.

Jim waited until the waiter filled Stevo's glass and left before he spoke. "I have never known you to take a day away from the store. But, to answer your question, I think Tom is a good man. He could be your son. Meaning, I think he has what it takes to run the store while you are away."

Stevo smiled, took a sip of his wine, then said, "Thanks, Jim. I needed an opinion from someone who is not a part of my close circle. Someone who would be honest and not say what they thought I wanted to hear."

"If you want honesty," continued Jim, "That new boy, Marjan, needs to learn English fast and not be so shy in the store."

Stevo didn't reply, just nodding. Jim was right.

Jim emptied his glass and said to Stevo, "I really need to get going."

Stevo finished his wine and before he could reach for his money, Jim put his money on the table, saying, "I am making some easy money because of you and Barbra. Speaking of Barbra, am I supposed to bow…kiss her hand?"

Stevo stood, saying, "Oh shut up. She will be unhappy with me for telling you what I did. Forget it and treat her as you have been."

Stevo waved goodbye to Jim Slade. In the store, he greeted a woman being helped by Tomo who was showing her an oak bookcase. Leaving them to complete their business, Stevo went into the kitchen, where Ignatz was cooking sausage he purchased at the Serbian Brothers' Market at 1724 Massachusetts. Stevo could smell the sauerkraut Ignatz would add to the sausage.

Without asking, Ignatz brought a cup of strong coffee to Stevo who smiled a "thank you".

They were alone in the kitchen, Stevo lost in his thoughts, thoughts about the future. Every now and then, Ignatz glanced at Stevo, concerned for the moodiness he sensed in the man he had come to regard as his friend.

The afternoon was almost gone and soon it would be time to close the store.

Barbra came into the kitchen, smiling, looking so happy. She had a lot of money and soon she and Josef would be in the house behind the tavern. Barbra looked especially nice in a cream-colored long dress with no cinched waist. It hung straight on her body with cream colored lace sewn down the front of the dress and at the wrist of her sleeves. As usual her strawberry-colored hair was piled atop her head, slightly loose above her ears.

To Ignatz she said, "That smells wonderful. Is that bratwurst?" She touched Stevo's shoulder as she passed him to her chair.

"I don't think so." said Ignatz, "I bought it at the Serbian Market. They make the sausage themselves."

Josef came into the kitchen, wearing a fresh shirt. No tie, with his sleeves rolled up. Barbra looked elegant, while he looked relaxed and casual.

To Barbra, he said, "Well, are you pleased with how the day went?"

She broke into a wide smile. "I haven't been this happy in a very long time." She looked from Stevo to Josef. She said, "For the first time since I can't remember when, I feel in control of my life."

To Stevo, she said, "Please be happy for us." She said this because Stevo seemed sad and lost in thought for the last few weeks.

"Of course I am happy for you both." said Stevo. "Do you know what you are going to do, once you get the house?"

This was the first Ignatz had heard of the house. He almost dropped the fork he was using with which to turn the sausage in the pan. "You are leaving us?" His voice was low. He couldn't understand not being with Barbra and Josef.

Barbra hadn't thought about Ignatz. She could see he was hurt. She said, "What will Stevo do if you left?"

Ignatz turned back to his stove, hoping he didn't show how hurt he felt.

Understanding Ignatz's feelings, Stevo said, "We will miss Ignatz terribly, but we will manage."

Tomo locked the store when the customer left, who was planning to return tomorrow, only making a down payment on the bookcase today.

Throughout the meal, there was a strained atmosphere. Barbra sensed Ignatz's hurt and was angry at herself for not thinking of him when they planned on buying the house.

Tomo sensed something was wrong, but didn't bother to ask, as he had something on his mind and wasn't sure how to tell Stevo about it.

The meal was finished with a plate of cheese and grapes with strong Turkish coffee after dinner.

The evening was cool with a refreshing breeze finding its way into the kitchen.

"Would you like to go for a walk?" Josef asked Barbra. She agreed and they went out the kitchen door into the pleasant, July evening.

Ignatz took a plate of food out to Bobo in the barn, and some meat scraps for Mali, who now it seems decided he wanted to belong to Bobo.

Looking at Tomo, Stevo said, "I sense you have something on your mind. Do you want to talk about it?"

Tomo, his handsome face troubled, offered Stevo a cigarette, before taking one himself. Stevo held a match for Tomo before lighting his own.

Tomo didn't know how to begin. He took a long drag on his cigarette.

"Well?" said Stevo waiting for Tomo to tell him what the problem is.

After a long loud sigh, Tomo said, "I have to get married."

"Who did you get pregnant?" demanded Stevo with all the concern a father would have.

"No one! I haven't held her hand or kissed her." said Tomo.

Stevo almost shouted, "What the hell are you talking about?"

"Marjan wants to marry Mara, but her father won't allow the marriage until the older sister, Julia is married." Tomo looked at Stevo knowing Stevo would think he was crazy. Then the young man said, "In order for Marjan and Mara to marry, I agreed to marry her older sister Julia."

CHAPTER 18

Two weeks passed and on the day of the wedding, three of Stevo's carriages were transporting the small wedding party to Sts. Peter & Paul Church in Whiting, where the parents of the brides preferred the service to take place.

An excited Marjan and Mara, along with Josef, who offered to be the Kum or Best Man, rode in one buggy. A somber Tomo, Julia, and Stevo were in the second buggy, while the very pleased parents of the brides to be, along with the two younger brothers, were in the third.

Stevo was not pleased with this marriage. Also, he was greatly disappointed in Tomo, who he had come to love and think of as a son. A couple days earlier, Tomo came home smelling of lilacs. Stevo said nothing, but remembered how annoyed Katya had been when Tomo spent the night with Grace. Tomo had not been out with Grace Adams for more than a year and now that he was getting married, he had obviously been to see her.

Sadness seemed to have overcome Stevo. He wasn't sure what he wanted to do, yet he had a vague plan for his own life, but people and events were a constant interruption.

The city of Gary and his store had lost all interest for him. When Milan was killed, it was as if his last strong tie to Katya had been severed. As outrageous and rude as Milan had been at times, he had become Stevo's closest friend.

Stevo remembered one night a few months ago when Milan came to the store after it had closed. Walking out in the yard where no one would overhear them, Milan had said, "Come with me to Yaga's. She has a couple of beauties from Chicago."

Stevo had not answered, he just looked at Milan.

Milan said, "I'll bet you haven't had any action since…since." He could not say the words, *since Katya died.* Instead, he slapped Stevo on the back and said, "What the hell! I'll even pay the dollar for her."

At the church, there were no pews filled with wedding guests. The priest stood at the altar behind the communion rail along with one altar boy.

It was a pretty church with lit candles throwing their flickering lights on the walls.

Depending on the viewer's conscience, the lovely statues of the Blessed Virgin, the Saints Peter and Paul, and Christ with his out stretched arms could appear to be loving or judgmental.

There was no organ music, no processional down the aisle. The two couples and their Kumovi stood outside the communion rail. The parents were seated in the first pew, beaming with joy. After all, they were sure their girls were marrying men with position and money.

The parents still owed the store for the cloth acquired for the bridal dresses, which the girls themselves had sewn, but the parents had been able to pay for the white shoes.

During the ceremony, Mara giggled a couple of times and Marjan had a huge grin on him face. Marjan wore his only nice suit with a white flower on his lapel.

Julia, not smiling, glanced nervously a few times at the somber Tomo. He was so very handsome. His light brown hair, his nicely trimmed moustache, and nicely arched brows over those dark eyes made her heart flutter. She found him the opposite of Marjan, who seemed immature.

After the communion was served, the brief ceremony was over. Everyone shook the priest's hand before leaving. That is all except Josef, who took the priest aside for a private conversation, while the others waited outside.

Outside, Mara and Julia's mother kissed both bridegrooms and gave them huge hugs. Tomo forced a smile and returned a hearty handshake to his father-in-law.

"You boys be good to our girls." said the father, wiping his wet eyes.

Stevo went through the motions of a happy participant, but he had other matters on his mind.

The conversation during the ride from Whiting to Milan's tavern was strained with many silences. Instead of being a happy bridegroom, Tomo appeared sullen and probably regretful for allowing himself to marry a stranger just so his brother could have the girl he loved.

At the back of Milan's Tavern, tables had been pushed together to make a long banquet table for the bridal party. Barbra picked wildflowers, such day lilies and Queen Anne's lace, making nice arrangements in large beer mugs setting four of them on the long table.

Ignatz was finished with the chickens he had been cooking in the yard, keeping the food warm for the wedding party. Both he and Mato were impressed seeing how efficiently Ivanka killed the chickens and had them plucked and cleaned in a short time.

When the brides and grooms, with their families, walked through the door of the tavern, applause greeted them. Even those who did not know them joined in the applause, as music greeted their arrival.

The parents of the brides, Marko and Mira Pavelich, with their two small sons, were impressed by the applause and the table set for them. They were poor people and everything seemed elegant to them.

Marko was a short, thin man, already graying. His wife Mira was not fat, but was round of body and face. Her very thin hair was pulled straight from her face into a tight bun at the back. One had to wonder how these two plain people produced such attractive daughters, especially Julia whose hazel eyes, smooth complexion, and golden brown hair made several of the men at the bar look to one another with approving nods.

Bottles of slivovitz and pitchers of beer were placed on the table, making Marko Pavelich's eyes widen in wonder. *Who was paying for this?*

The atmosphere in the bar was full of gaiety. Men at the bar held up their drinks toasting the brides and grooms. The noise level rose as the meal progressed, and especially when Ignatz put a plate of chicken pieces on the bar to share with the men standing there.

"Mnogo hvala…thank you." The men at the bar said to the father of the brides, assuming he was paying for the wedding feast.

When the meal was finished, but the table not completely cleared, Ivanka went to the banquet table with two aprons in her hands. She had proudly sewn them on her new sewing machine. The white aprons had two large pockets sewn on each of them. Ivanka asked the girls to stand up while she tied the aprons around each of them.

The men at the bar, already feeling in a wedding party mood, knew what the aprons were for and shouted their approval.

Ivanka nudged Tomo and nodded that he and Julia should dance first, with Mara and Marjan following.

Tomo took Julia by the hand and danced the first dance. Before their dance was completed, Marjan and Mara danced. When their dance was finished, the men at the bar lined up to dance with the brides. Before starting to dance, the men placed money in the apron pockets. This was meant for the bride to keep, usually for the arrival of a baby.

Unnoticed, Josef found Barbra in the kitchen of the living quarters.

"Come," he said, "I want to talk to you."

With a puzzled look, not understanding what could be so important, Barbra wiped her hands on a towel, tossing it on the table.

Josef was a strong man, slightly grey at the temples, usually his blue eyes were sharp, but around Barbra he had been quiet and self-restrained, only in the background, never assertive.

Then, he took Barbra firmly by the arm and led her into the house behind the tavern which Barbra had purchased.

As they reached the side door, the one leading to what had been Ivanka's room, where Barbra now slept, Barbra asked, "What is the matter? Has something happened?"

The room was still furnished as Ivanka had it. Barbra had yet to properly decorate the house. She sat on the small bed while Josef sat on the straight back wooden chair facing her.

Before she could speak, Josef said, "I spoke with the priest at the church."

Barbra's eyes widened. She didn't know where his words were leading.

"There is no way we can get married in the church." he said.

At these words, Barbra's mouth fell open. No words came out. She only stared at him.

He continued, "Since Stefan abandoned you and married someone else without a divorce, you must have an annulment."

Still speechless, Barbra stared at Josef who said, "The priest said that he positively could not marry us."

Barbra looked into Josef's eyes for a long time, not speaking. She looked deep into them. When she spoke she said, "I never knew you cared that much for me."

Now it was Josef's turn to be surprised. He said, "How could you not know? For two years I comforted you and took care of you when you lost the babies." He paused looking at her for some reaction to his words. He said, "I locked my office door and came to America with you." Again he asked, "How could you not know?"

In a small, low voice Barbra said, "You never said anything to me. Not one word to let know how you really felt."

Josef leaned forward, his eyes earnest, "How could I? I had to respect the fact that you were married. When you decided to follow Stefan to America, I could only think you still loved him."

A tear trailed down Barbra's cheek, she said, "I haven't loved him for a very long time. I was honoring the fact that he was my husband."

"I want to be your husband," said Josef, "but I can't for a while." He looked at her and asked, "Would you marry me, once we get matters straightened out?"

Barbra reached her hand out and took his, pulling him to her. Josef wasn't sure what was happening, but let himself be wrapped in her arms.

Her tender kiss became passionate and it let loose both their reserves. They had each been holding back in a sense of honor and now it no longer mattered.

Barbra's husband, Stefan, had been very experienced in sex, having visited Magda's girls often, but with all his experience, he never made Barbra feel the love she felt from Josef. With tenderness and gentleness, Josef made her feel as if she were the only woman he ever loved, filling her with emotions she never had with Stefan.

So, there in a partially furnished room, in broad daylight, Barbra and Josef, without words pledged themselves to one another forever.

CHAPTER 19

That evening, the wedding party concluded after much kissing from the girls and all the goodbyes, the Pavelich parents were driven to their home by Bobo.

The sleeping arrangements at the store were now Marjan and Mara in the loft above the kitchen, where Ignatz had slept, now available since he was at the house behind the tavern with Barbra and Josef. Julia and Tomo were in the room off to the side of the kitchen. Originally, that room had been Stevo's before he built the second floor above the store.

Stevo had so much on his mind. His nights were filled with dreams about his dead father. The dreams disturbed him, for it was only since Milan's death that Stevo's father came to him almost each night. More disturbing than the dreams were the times he awoke in the middle of the night thinking he heard his father's voice calling, "Aide, Stevo…Come, Stevo."

Stevo remembered how Katya would talk about the visitors in her dreams and she seemed to know what those visits meant. Strange, Stevo thought, he had not dreamt about Katya in what seemed like a long time.

In his dreams, Stevo and his father would go on the fishing boats just as they had when they lived in New Orleans. Several times during these dreams, Stevo would awaken, sit up in his bed, and be overwhelmed with the scents of the flowers in the courtyard where they had lived on Canal Street, not far from the Mississippi River.

Stevo felt as if he was intruding sitting in his own kitchen, hearing Marjan and Mara in the loft laughing, making sounds of lovemaking. However, there were no such sounds from Tomo and Julia's room, just off the kitchen.

Stevo went out onto the small sitting area outside the kitchen door. He sat in a chair looking up at the starlit night.

The sky was clear, the moon was shining brightly and the soft breeze was pleasant.

Before lighting a cigarette, Stevo took a deep breath of the fresh night air. Instead of smelling gardenias, oleanders, or magnolias, the smells of New Orleans, Stevo smelled only mint, which was planted in a pot next to the kitchen door.

Stevo heard movement in the kitchen. Through the open door, Stevo could make out Tomo, with a wine bottle and glass in his hand, sitting at the kitchen table. Before Stevo could call out to Tomo, he saw the figure of Julia wearing a long, cotton night gown, come to the table. Stevo could see her standing and looking at Tomo for a long while, not speaking.

Tomo filled the glass with wine and pushed it across the table towards Julia as he took a long drink from the bottle.

Stevo, sensing this was a very private moment, sat very still. He knew he should not be listening, but felt he couldn't let himself be known. Something serious was going on between Julia and Tomo.

Julia, her hair in one long braid hanging down the front of her nightgown, picked up the wine glass. She raised the glass in a toast, "To my husband." She said sarcastically.

Tomo took another drink from the wine bottle, saying nothing.

The shaft of moonlight illuminated the dark kitchen enough for Stevo to see Julia as she sat in a chair across from Tomo.

Tomo said nothing, but Julia continued to speak. "Don't take whatever anger you have out on me. Be angry at yourself for marrying me just so your baby brother could marry my baby sister." She took another sip of the wine. "It was your choice."

Tomo's head jerked up, facing Julia. "That's right." she said, "We both married for them. But," she went on, "at least you appealed to me. I saw how kind you were to my mother that day when you brought my brother home from the mill in the casket. And I thought you were polite to my father when you came with Marjan, agreeing to marry me so that he and Mara could marry."

Tomo still said nothing, he only looked at Julia. This was the first time he heard her speak in such a personal manner. Until now, they had only greeted each other politely at the meeting when Mato agreed to the marriage.

She went on, "When we were in the church, I looked at you and thought how lucky I was to have such a handsome husband."

Still not speaking, Tomo reached for her glass and filled it with more wine.

Drinking nearly half the wine, Julia, her eyes bright, perhaps from the beginning of tears or the wine, said, "My parents thought my brother was so special, because he was the first born and a male."

She put down her glass, rubbed her eyes with her fists. "All I was to my parents was someone to take care of the younger children. When we first came to America, we went to some relatives in Texas." She looked hard at Tomo saying, "Do you know what I was doing there from the time I was seven years old? I picked cotton until my little fingers bled. I had to look after Mara when she played on the porch. I was killing the snakes that made their way up between the boards onto the porch."

She picked up the glass and finished the wine. Putting the glass down, she gave Tomo a hard look saying, "I was nothing to my parents. My brother was everything. I went as far as the fourth grade and learned to read and write and do figures.

Look at me Tomo." she demanded. "I am not ugly. I am smart, I am a hard worker." Julia pointed to sounds coming from the loft, "If you don't want me for that...at least treat me with the respect a good wife deserves."

Now Tomo really looked at Julia. He was seeing a person, a person of worth.

Julia was not finished speaking. "I will never shame you. I will work at your side here at the store. Mara can do the cooking, that's all she is good for, except maybe what she is doing up there." Julia rolled her eyes upward. "Just show me what to do in the store and I can do it. And if you want other women, then, just don't shame me with it."

Tomo rose from his chair. He looked at the still seated Julia. There was fire in this 16-year-old. She was mature beyond her years. *This is a woman*, he thought.

Tomo went to where Julia was sitting. He took both her hands and pulled her to her feet. He took her in his arms and kissed her, gently at first. When he felt her respond, his kissing became passionate. Because of what those kisses were conveying and the fire they were building, Tomo picked up Julia and carried her into their room.

Stevo heard Tomo kick the bedroom door shut. He no longer felt guilty for having listened to their private conversation. Stevo was sure he liked Julia and he was also sure she would be a good wife for Tomo.

Stevo smoked his cigarette, looked again at the stars and the moon and wondered about his own future. There were so many details and obstacles to be taken care of and to overcome.

Finished with his cigarette, he ground the butt into the flower pot of growing mint. Quietly, he closed the kitchen door, walking softly, so as not to be heard. He gently opened the door leading into the store. As he climbed the stairs up to his room, he wondered if he would again dream of his father.

CHAPTER 20

The following morning, Stevo was having his morning coffee seated again at the table outside the kitchen door.

It was obvious to him that his kitchen and home were no longer his. Instead of Stevo's usual quiet mornings when he could read his various newspapers and sip his coffee in peace, there was now the bickering of two sisters and two brothers.

Julia was annoyed with Mara for not coming down sooner to help with breakfast, while Tomo wanted his brother down earlier to discuss the tasks for the day.

Stevo got up from the table, walked the three steps to the door, pulling it shut with a loud slam. He couldn't handle all the loud conversations over what appeared, to him, to be trivial matters.

Stevo was dressed in dark blue gabardine trousers, a cream-colored shirt without the stiff collar attached, for he was not planning to work that day. As he rolled up his shirt sleeves, his eye caught Katya's wedding ring, always on the little finger of his right hand. Seeing the ring made him remember what fun it was to have her in the kitchen and later in the apartment above. Katya and Cleona had made him smile often, though he pretended to be annoyed with their excitement and preparations for their Royal cosmetics. But most of all, the ring reminded him how empty his life had become without love. Katya's love had made life so interesting, the conflicts, the surprises, and most of all the laughter.

Lost in his thoughts, Stevo did not hear Barbra and Josef come through the gate to the table.

Josef saw the closed kitchen door. "Giving the young married kids some privacy?" he asked.

Stevo extended his hand for them to sit, as he said, "I closed the door to give me privacy. There is too much bickering and loud talk for me this early in the day." He asked, "How about some coffee?"

He started to rise to call for coffee, but Barbra motioned for him to stay. Dressed in her pale green day dress with matching scarf, she opened the door hearing the loud conversations and immediately understood Stevo's annoyance.

Seeing Barbra, the room went quiet. She smiled, noticing the stares from the four of them. She called out from the door, "Some coffee for Josef and me, and more for Stevo."

In seconds, a smiling Julia, dressed in a peasant skirt and blouse, appeared with cups for the coffee and a plate of warm bread and cheese. Behind her came shy Mara, dressed the same as her sister, with the coffee pot in one hand and the pot of warm milk in the other. She poured them together in each cup, pleased that she didn't spill any of it.

When Mara started through the kitchen door, Stevo called out, "Close that door!"

As the three sipped their coffees and nibbled at the cheese, Stevo noticed a change in Barbra and Josef. Both of their faces were relaxed, happy, almost glowing.

Stevo realized why the change. They were happy. He was sure they had at last found one another in a way they had not before. He hoped he was right and if so, it pleased him greatly for he liked them both very much.

In the past, Josef did not take the lead, but now he was the first to speak. "Stevo, you know Barbra bought the house behind the tavern. We need furniture, but we don't have much money left." He looked at Stevo for some reaction, seeing none he continued, "I have some money in a Zagreb bank and I have items in my office which could be sold."

Barbra broke in saying, "My store," for she no longer claimed it to be Stefan's, "has many pieces of art and furniture which could also be sold."

Stevo was silent for a long time…thinking. He wanted to help these two who he had come to be so very fond of, but…

He stood up, going to the kitchen door. Opening it, he looked around for Tomo, catching Tomo's eye, Stevo motioned for him to come outside.

With Tomo at his side he said, "Come talk with us. You may not want to open the store today."

Puzzled by this remark, Tomo followed Stevo, stopping to shake hands with Josef and Barbra.

There wasn't a fourth chair, so Tomo, not yet in his good work suit, upended an empty barrel and sat on it.

To Josef, Stevo said, "Tell Tomo what you just told me."

Again, Josef repeated what he and Barbra needed and about what assets they had in Zagreb.

Tomo, looking confused, turned to Stevo asking, "What do you want to do?"

Stevo offered his pack of cigarettes to Josef, who took one. He then offered the pack to Tomo, who declined. No one spoke as Stevo offered a light to Josef and then lit his own cigarette.

Tomo asked again, "What do you want to do?"

Stevo said softly, "It is not what I want to do, but what you want to do." He paused, looking at Tomo, "I am selling the store to you."

Tomo's face went pale, while Josef and Barbra gasped in surprise.

Blowing a plume of smoke into the air, Stevo only looked at the three across the table from him.

When no one spoke, Stevo said, "The store and Gary no longer mean anything to me. Katya is gone, Milan is gone…I need to go somewhere, away from my sadness."

As if on cue, a dog howled mournfully somewhere in the distance.

Josef, Barbra, Tomo, and Stevo took the street car to the Gary State Bank at Fifth Avenue and Broadway, one of the city's proudest cement buildings. At one time the builders of Gary referred to it as Cement City because they felt cement and steel combined would make for strong lasting structures.

Stevo made no explanations to his companions. This confused them. Yet, they all had confidence in him and did not press him with questions.

When Stevo led the way through the bank entrance, several seated clerks stood at their desks and greeted him. This surprised Tomo, for he had never been to the bank with Stevo.

Stevo shook hands with Mr. White, the nicely-dressed bank manager, wearing a navy blue suit. He then introduced Mr. White to Barbra and Josef. The banker had seen Tomo in the bank several times. They were all invited into a private enclosed area of the bank where they were seated.

"First," began Stevo, "my friends," he nodded towards Barbra and Josef, have assets at a bank in Zagreb. What can you do to transfer those assets to your bank?"

Without hesitation, the banker said, "There are American branch banks now in Europe, with proper information we could have the money transferred, after the monetary conversion is made. It won't be right away…well I can't really say how long it will take." He looked apologetic, "Hopefully, no less than a month. Come this way, please." he said to Barbra and Josef as he led them to a nearby clerk. Barbra and Josef sat in the offered chairs.

"Miss Jenkins will assist you and help with the proper paperwork." said the bank manager, before returning to Stevo and Tomo.

When Mr. White was back at his desk, Stevo said, "I will be withdrawing some money soon and later when I know where I will be, I will contact you to transfer the rest of my money."

The bank manager frowned and Tomo looked worried and sad. Mr. White said, "Mr. Markovich, we will hate to lose such a valued bank customer."

Stevo did not reply to the banker's comment, instead he said, "I want to establish a line of credit for this young man, Tomo Mandich."

"Why yes, of course." said Mr. White, "We know Mr. Mandich, not as well as we know you, but he has been a customer here for a while."

Stevo smiled, "I plan to negotiate a private sale of my store to Mr. Mandich. I will carry the note, but as I won't be here, I want the bank to handle the payments in my name."

Tomo was feeling many emotions. Sadness at losing Stevo and fear for the future. He wondered, *Did he know enough? Was he smart enough to handle the store on his own? Where would he get good, honest employees*? So many thoughts were in his mind.

Digging through his desk drawers, Mr. White pulled out some forms. He put them in a large brown envelope saying, "When you have filled in the all the terms and dates necessary, bring these back in and we will proceed from there." He looked at Tomo, "I would like you both here so that we can have the signatures witnessed."

Leaving the bank, Stevo suggested they go to the Gary Hotel for some refreshments. For a moment Stevo thought Barbra might remember seeing Stefan there with Adele

Manning, but Barbra said brightly, "I would love to see the dining room."

Barbra was impressed with the elegant room. She saw white tablecloths and palm plants near the windows which were adorned with dark red velvet drapes, tied back with golden-tasseled cords. The chairs were medallion backed, covered in the same red velvet as the drapes.

During the lunch of chicken pot pie and a piece of American apple pie, Barbra and Josef were cheerful. Life was looking brighter for them.

It was Tomo who was unusually quiet. He had no appetite. It seemed to him that his life was upended within 24 hours. He was now a married man. He was now totally in charge of the store. He would soon be making monthly payments on the store, and worst of all his brother Marjan was nowhere near ready to work in the store. Tomo wondered, *Could he handle all of these responsibilities?*

Back at the store, Barbra and Josef said their thanks and walked back to their house behind the tavern.

In the kitchen, Tomo took Julia by the hand. With a puzzled look on her face, she followed him to their bedroom. He closed the door and told her where they had been and what Stevo was proposing to do.

Julia looked at Tomo. His face showed his worry. She asked, "What will happen if we cannot make the monthly payments?"

In a low voice, Tomo said, "Then I suppose it means we lose the store."

Stevo went up to the second floor above the store. He walked from room to room, memories flooding his mind. In his bedroom, he looked at the side table where Katya's gypsy bracelet and her Nona's large red coral cameo rested.

He went to the end of the hall to Katya's small indoor chapel. He usually only sat on the pew, but today he kneeled. With his hands over his face, he sobbed for the life he had made for himself and was soon to leave.

When Barbra and Josef were about to enter the side door of their house, they heard what sounded like a man begging. Looking at the back entrance of the living quarters of the tavern, they saw Stanko Perpich, the man Ivanka came to join in America. In his arms was a bundle.

Josef and Barbra watched in wonder as they heard the door slam shut. Stanko turned away, startled that someone had witnessed his humiliation.

"What is wrong? Can we help?" asked Josef.

Barbra approached the man. He looked gaunt and almost ill with worry.

Almost sobbing, he said, "The baby is two weeks old." His voice caught, "My wife died a few days ago. I can't find anyone to take the baby. I am leaving for Pittsburgh to be with my cousin."

Barbra reached for the bundle taking it out of his arms. She lifted the blanket, revealing its face. She thought the baby was beautiful. Josef was at her side, wanting to see if the baby looked well.

"What is it," she asked, "a boy or girl?"

"A boy." said Stanko.

Barbra looked up into Josef's face and he smiled at her, saying to Stanko, "We will take him."

A look of relief came over Stanko' s face.

He grabbed one of Barbra's hands and kissed it several times. He then did the same to Josef.

Before they could change their minds, Stanko, backing away, bowed until he reached the road where he took off in a run.

Looking at the baby, Josef said, "He didn't tell us the baby's name."

"We will call him Josef." said Barbra.

CHAPTER 21

Stevo woke later than usual. He stayed up the night before catching up on his newspaper and magazine reading in bed.

For some reason, having the two sisters in the house made it seem more crowded. This was strange because Stevo didn't feel that way when Josef and Barbra and Ignatz were staying with him. It was even quieter then. Now, instead of speaking in soft tones, he felt the girls were yelling instead of talking.

Stevo looked out the one window in his room which overlooked the yard. He saw Bobo with a bucket of water washing the wheels on one of the carriages. By the sun's shadows on the neighboring roof top, Stevo guessed it was around nine o'clock.

He sat in the comfortable chair next to a side table. The table where Katya's bracelet and coral cameo rested.

His dream from the night before came to him as vividly as if it had been real. He was a boy of about 16 with his father going to the docks to net shrimp. Seated in the boat, his father sat across from Stevo with pride in his eyes, as he looked at him.

Stevo reached for the pack of Camels he bought at the Gary Hotel the day before. It wasn't that these were his new favorite cigarettes, but seeing them on the counter reminded him of Milan. It was Milan who first shared them with him.

He took a match from the ceramic match holder and struck it on the rough sides of the holder. He lit the cigarette and inhaled deeply while surveying the room.

Stevo wondered...*Will I miss this room? Will I miss the store?*

After dressing in casual clothes instead of a suit, he went downstairs. The lights in the store were still dark.

Mara and Julia greeted him. He answered with a "Dobro Yutro," walking to the outside table.

Stevo was starting to like this outdoor table. He was not bothered here with chatter and questions. He missed Ignatz, who seemed to anticipate Stevo's needs and quietly delivered coffee or wine without being asked.

It was a very nice morning. A gentle breeze touched Stevo as he sat in the shaded part of the yard. A sparrow perched on the chair near Stevo, its little head jerking back and forth. It seemed to be greeting Stevo with little chirps, or perhaps it was looking for some bread crumbs to take back to its nest. The little bird flew away at the sound of the gate opening.

Josef came into yard, alone. "Dobro yutro...good morning." he said when he saw Stevo at the table.

"Dobro yutro." replied Stevo. "Come," he motioned to the chair the bird flew away from, "have some breakfast with me." Stevo looked at the gate asking, "Where is Barbra?"

"She is home with the baby." said Josef, smiling at Julia, who had heard him and was coming through the door anticipating he would want coffee.

Stevo looked at Josef bewildered. He said, "She never looked pregnant."

Josef laughed realizing Stevo assumed Barbra gave birth to the baby.

"No." said Josef, smiling. "A man gave us the baby."

Stevo still looked puzzled, so Josef explained, "A man came to the back door of the tavern, where he was ignored. When we saw him start to leave, we noticed he was holding a baby." Josef stirred sugar into his coffee as he said, "He told us his wife died and he was leaving for Pittsburgh and no one would take the baby."

Stevo said, "So, Barbra, who has lost two babies, wanted the baby."

"We both did." said Josef. "The baby makes us feel like a family."

Stevo said nothing for a few moments. He could understand the life Josef and Barbra wanted and he envied them.

"I'm happy for you both." said Stevo sincerely. "In the back of the store we have a crib. Let me make it the first gift for the baby."

Josef reached across the table taking Stevo's hand in his saying, "Thank you, my first and best friend in America!"

Hearing Tomo's voice through the open door, Stevo said, "Let's talk with Tomo about the furniture you need for the house."

Without being called, Tomo came out to the table. "Julia said you were here. Good Morning." He looked around, "You came without Barbra?"

Stevo said, "Sit down Tomo. Josef wants to talk about furnishing the house and make some arrangements about payments." Stevo looked at Josef, "Am I correct in assuming that is why you are here?"

After Julia brought more coffee and a plate of warm bread sprinkled generously with sugar, she left the men to talk.

Brushing away the sugar that fell from the bread onto his shirt, Josef said, "I plan to be a doctor again. I don't know what certification I will need, but I am confident I can get it."

Both Stevo and Tomo looked at Josef with great interest, as he went on. "I plan on making the first two rooms of the house into an office waiting room and the one across the hall into an examination room."

Tomo was the first to speak, "I think that is wonderful. We need a Croatian doctor, one of our own." He thought for a moment, "You will need a desk, chairs, tables, and filing cabinets. Wait here." He went into the house to get pencil and paper.

Back at the table, he began to write down the already mentioned items. Looking up he said, "You will need household furnishings. Oh, yes, and a well-furnished kitchen for Ignatz."

"And", said Stevo with a big smile, "a rocking chair for the Momma. I have already promised a crib as my gift."

Tomo looked up asking, "Barbra is going to have a baby?"

Laughing Stevo said, "She already has one."

Josef said, "We took a baby from a man whose wife died."

Tomo nodded, "That must be the Perpich baby. The mother died recently. We buried her. Remember?" he asked Stevo.

Stevo nodded, "Yes, I remember." He also remembered that it was Perpich that Ivanka had soundly slapped at Milan's. Stevo figured that Stanko Perpich was hoping Ivanka would take the baby. He said nothing about Ivanka or Stanko to Josef.

Stevo and Josef watched as the list of items on Tomo's paper was getting longer and longer. With a worried look, Josef turned to Stevo, who showed no concern.

Tomo stood with the paper in his hand. "Let's go see which pieces you want delivered."

"Sit down." said Josef, "We need to discuss terms. Barbra and I have no money. No money yet. We have no idea when my money will be transferred from Zagreb." He then turned to Stevo asking, "Would you give me the address in Trieste of Katya's mother?" Seeing the surprised look on Stevo's face, Josef continued, "Katya's mother Sophie and her husband, the attorney Alexie Lukas, came to my office in Zagreb. Since Alexie is a lawyer, I want to hire him to dispose of my office in Zagreb and the items in the store Barbra and Stefan had. The buildings are very near to each other."

"Of course I will give you the address. In fact, I will also write to him on your behalf." said Stevo.

To Tomo, Josef said, "Let me work for you until our money from Zagreb arrives."

"We will talk about that later." said Tomo.

Josef had no more to say, so he and Tomo stood to go into the store. Seeing that Stevo made no move to accompany them, the two men went in without him.

Stevo sipped his coffee, bit into the sugared bread and wondered if he could start a new life somewhere else, just as Barbra and Josef and so many others have done.

The little sparrow flew back, this time landing on the ground where it found some bread crumbs. Seeing the bird, Stevo broke pieces of the sugared bread and dropped them near the bird. Seeing the bread, the bird greedily grabbed a piece in its beak and flew away, only to return soon for more.

Stevo picked up a Chicago newspaper, thumbed through it. Nothing caught his interest. He turned to the back pages and came across the train schedules. This caught his eye. After reading through the train destinations, Stevo folded the paper, placing it on the table. Josef and Tomo, busy picking out furniture, never noticed Stevo climb the stairs to his room.

In his room, Stevo opened the doors to the chifferobe. He took out Katya's hanging dresses and put them on the bed. Next, he pulled out the drawers and removed what folded items were in them.

Thinking that Barbra might be the same size as Katya had been, he took the blue lace dress and the silver dress she had worn on New Year's Eve and folded them neatly. He didn't have a box to put them in, so he pulled a pillow case from the bed and placed the neatly folded garments in it. He looked at what was left on the bed and thought Ivanka could use them.

He looked around and wanted something for Cleona. Cleona was small and thin. He wondered if the maroon dress with the maroon lace collar Katya had worn to the meeting to raise money for the Croatian Church would please her.

With the pillow case filled with the dresses, Stevo went back into the store. Josef and Tomo were still picking out items for the new house.

As he walked through the kitchen, he saw Mara stretching out dough for strudel. To Julia he said, "Please bring a bottle of wine and some glasses to the table outside."

He set the pillowcase on the tabletop before walking out to the stable.

Bobo, brushing a horse, saw him approaching and called out, "Morning, Mr. Steve."

"Good Morning, Bobo." said Stevo as he ran his hand across the back of his favorite black horse. Motioning to the shed, where Bobo lived, Stevo said, "Let's go inside. I have something to tell you."

A look of concern showed on Bobo's face. He had worked for Stevo from the first day Stevo opened the store. He could usually tell when Stevo was worried or burdened with a problem.

Stevo looked around the interior of the shed. It was tidy and clean. The sleeping cot was made up, towels neatly folded next to the wash bowl and pitcher. There was even a rag rug next to the bed.

Bobo offered Stevo the only chair in the room, while he sat on the bed. "Is something wrong, Mr. Steve?" he asked.

Stevo said, "I'm selling the store to Tomo."

Bobo thought about this for a moment then asked, "Why is that?"

"I'm going away." He said, looking at his friend and employee.

"Is it them boys and their brides that makin you leave?" asked Bobo.

Stevo smiled. That wasn't the reason, but he would be pleased to be away from them. "No." he said. "The store doesn't mean anything to me anymore." He looked at his old friend, "Not since Katya is gone…and Milan."

"No sir." agreed Bobo, "Nothing is the same."

They both sat not talking for a while. Bobo broke the silence saying, "So what happens to me now, Mr. Steve? Will I be leavin too?"

"No!" Stevo answered firmly. "I have it in the sales contract that you stay here for the rest of your life or until you decide to leave."

With wonder in his eyes, Bobo said, "You did that for me, Mr. Steve? Did you really do that?"

"Yes I did. But, I didn't have to. What would Tomo do without you? You are just as valuable to him as you have been to me." said Stevo sincerely. "I am selling the store to Tomo."

Coming from the stable, Stevo saw Josef and Tomo at the table discussing the pieces they chose and both agreed it would take more than one trip for the enclosed carriage on wheels to transport everything.

Stevo sat at the table opening the wine, while listening to the conversation. Stevo felt that Tomo was handling the transaction well.

Stevo poured the wine into each of the three glasses, waiting for the conversation to end, before taking a sip.

He looked at Tomo and thought of him as the son he and Katya could have had. After all, he came to Katya's house when he was 15, escaping from a bondage agreement to work on a farm in Crown Point. From that day to the day she died,

Katya cared for Tomo as if he were her younger brother or her son.

When the furniture transaction appeared completed, Stevo pushed the wine glasses towards each of the men. He raised his own in a toast, "To the future." he said. Only he knew what the toast meant.

Josef left and it was now well past noon. Stevo stayed at the table, waiting for Tomo to return from giving instructions to Bobo for the next day's delivery.

When Tomo returned, Stevo poured him more wine. He looked at Tomo a long time, until Tomo became uncomfortable.

Tomo asked, "What is the matter? Why are you looking at me that way?"

Instead of answering him, Stevo said, "Let's go to the bank this afternoon and sign the papers for the sale of the store."

Tomo's jaw dropped. "Why today? Can't it wait?"

"It must be today." said Stevo. "I want to leave tomorrow. I will be leaving Gary."

Tomo's eyes filled with tears. "You can't leave." he was almost pleading. "What will I do without you?" He reached across the table grabbing Stevo's hands.

With understanding and deep feeling for the young man, Stevo said, "You will be fine. I was a year younger than you are now when I started this store. You learned from me and from working here." He squeezed Tomo's hand, "You will do better than I have."

The next day, there was no chattering, no arguing between the sisters in the kitchen. Even Marjan was worried about their futures without Stevo to control things.

Before sunlight, Stevo saddled and rode his favorite horse, Rona, to the cemetery. This was the first time he rode the horse to visit the graves. He usually walked.

Today, he sat between Katya's grave and Milan's, talking to them, telling them where he was going and why. As always, he kissed his finger tips and touched Katya's gravestone. This time he did the same to Milan's stone.

Back in his room, Stevo gathered up what clothes of Katya's were left and bundled them up for Bobo to give to Ivanka when he went to deliver the furniture to Josef.

In his small hand valise, he put Katya's gypsy bracelet and the coral cameo which had belonged to her grandmother in Trieste. He went to the tiny chapel and took Katya's blue rosary from the marble top. Next to the altar was a chalk figure of the Madonna. Stevo lifted the figure up and found what he was looking for, the Cheroots cigar box holding some money. It was the same cigar box he found hidden in the wall of his stepmother's home in New Orleans. It was the money in the box which helped Stevo start the Markovich Furniture Store.

Tomo insisted on driving Stevo to the train station in their best buggy. The young man was so sick to his stomach with sadness that he did not open the store that morning. A sign was on the door in English and Croatian: CLOSED ~ ZATVORENO.

With the luggage in the back, Stevo held Katya's green dress folded in his arms. Tomo stopped in front of the house Katya had once owned, the house where Tomo lived with Katya and her first husband, Ivan.

Stevo went to the back of the house alone to say goodbye to this wonderful lady who was Katya's business partner and nurse during her illness.

Cleona was in back chasing the goats out of her vegetable garden when she saw Stevo near the back stairs.

"Mr. Steve." she called out. "What brings you here, something wrong?"

As she walked closer, she saw the green dress. "What you doin with that dress?" she asked, concern showing in her eyes.

Stevo noticed the back porch was the same, with witch hazel branches and other flowers scattered about, drying.

Again she asked, "What you doin with that dress?"

"I brought it for you." he said. "I wanted you to have something of Katya's."

"I already got her house." said Cleona, her eyes narrowing, "Why you givin me the dress?"

Stevo pushed the dress into Cleona's hands saying, "I am leaving Gary. I sold the store to Tomo and I am leaving now."

Grasping the dress in one hand, the little black woman wrapped her free arm around Stevo. "Oh, Mr. Steve, Mr. Steve, why? What will we do without you?"

She hung onto his arm with her free hand, the other holding the dress. She was sobbing. "Will you come back?"

When he didn't answer she looked up at him asking, "Where you goin, Mr. Steve?"

"Home." he said softly.

CHAPTER 22

Tomo was heartsick driving Stevo in the carriage to the downtown train station. Most of the ride was without conversation, both men lost in their thoughts. When the train station was in sight, Tomo said, "Stevo...Stevo, I don't know how I will do it on my own. You have always been in charge."

He looked at Stevo seeing tenderness in his best friend's eyes. Stevo said, "Don't worry, Tomo. You will do just fine. I wouldn't be leaving you if I didn't think you could handle it. Just get your brother to learn English and learn more about the business." Both of Tomo's hands were holding the reins, so Stevo patted Tomo's knee. He said, "You have a good wife there. She will be a lot of help to you, if you let her."

With his luggage on the station platform, Stevo hugged Tomo, who had tears in his eyes. Stevo said, "I don't think I could love you more if you were my real son."

The train for Chicago was pulling into the station at Third & Broadway. Stevo had his ticket, watched the porters put his luggage on the train, and gave Tomo a last hug.

Tomo stood at the station until the train was out of sight.

From the Gary train station, Stevo went to Chicago to the passenger terminal with the entrance at West Madison St. It was a large and impressive building and considered to be a truly modern structure for the time.

Stevo had his steamer trunk, which stood upright with clothes hanging on one side and folded shirts and other small items in the four drawers on the other side, one leather suitcase, and the valise with money and important papers.

At the Chicago train station, he arrived in time to buy a ticket for the New York, Chicago, and St. Louis train. It was also known as the Nickel Plate. Stevo wanted to go to St.

Louis. There he would board the *Princess*, a paddle wheel steamboat that traveled down the Mississippi.

When he arrived at the St. Louis station, he caught a motorized taxi to the boat dock. Stevo boarded the *Princess* early and was given a sleeping room on the second deck.

The Princess was 150-feet long and burned wood. Leaving St. Louis it had a good stock of wood, but during the trip on the Mississippi, it would make several stops to get more and to drop off cargo from the north. The door to Stevo's private room opened out onto the second level deck. He leaned on the rail to see all the busy activity on the dock in the preparation of leaving.

Looking down he saw nicely dressed women with their parasols, some to board the ship and others just to say goodbye. Taxis, along with horse drawn carriages, crowded the dock, unloading people and luggage. The traffic sounds, shouts, laughter, and the clip clop of horse hooves all drifted up to the where Stevo stood.

Already Stevo could tell the difference in the smells of the St. Louis riverfront from those of Gary. There were smells of the water, burning wood, fish, and wild plants along the riverfront mixed with the aroma of frying chicken from a nearby restaurant.

St. Louis grew in construction, businesses, schools, and population after the Civil War. There were still some native trees, mainly oak, maple, hickory, and flowering dogwood, very similar to the Ozarks. Many trees would soon be gone due to the growing population.

An eagle lazily floated overhead before heading for the wooded area. There were some gulls circling above the boat, swooping into the water for fish. Somewhere Stevo heard the quacking of ducks, but didn't see any.

This was to be an eight-day river trip. Stevo had a young, black porter, perhaps no more that 16 years old, bring him a dinner of fried fish and vegetables to his room. Stevo didn't want to make pleasant conversation with fellow passengers. He left his cabin door open for the fresh air. He was starting a new venture in his life and wanted to think about it. Most of all, he wasn't sure what he wanted to do, or why there was this strong pull within him to return to New Orleans.

As he ate the fried bass, his thoughts drifted to the dreams he had been having. His wife Katya, when she was alive, always seemed to know what dreams meant. Now he wondered what the one dream of Katya and Milan, standing side-by–side, smiling at Stevo meant. Then there were the many dreams of Stevo with his father. Only recently had his father been coming to him in dreams. In some dreams, he, as a young boy, and his father were on fishing boats together. In other dreams, he and his father were walking home after a day of netting crabs. But lately, his dreams were of a now adult Stevo walking with his father, into the courtyard of what had been their home in New Orleans. This particular dream seemed to repeat itself often. But more disturbing than the dreams were the nights Stevo thought he heard his father calling to him.

Stevo passed the days on the boat mostly alone. Smiling and speaking when spoken to, but he avoided shipboard companions. He was enjoying the solitude. Most of his time was spent reading the local newspapers brought to him with each stopping of the boat. The young porter would bring whatever papers and magazines he could find. He even brought Stevo two books left by passengers from a previous voyage. Stevo couldn't have chosen two more different, yet still enjoyable books, had he tried. The first was *John Barleycorn: Alcoholic Memoirs* by Jack London and the second was *The Return of Tarzan* by Edgar Rice Burroughs. He finished reading the two books within three days.

The various newspapers informed Stevo that Ghandi had left South Africa after leading a passive resistance. Another paper had a mention that the Boston Braves began their drive from last to first place in the National League.

It seemed to Stevo the world was going mad when he read: "*Irish Volunteers unload a shipment of 1,500 rifles and 45,000 rounds of ammunition. These arrived from Germany aboard Erskin Childers' yacht the Asgard. British troops fired on the jeering crown on Batchelors Walk, Bublin, killing three citizens.*"

What caught Stevo's attention was a July 28 headline. It confirmed what Stevo had been thinking about; war in Europe. Austria had declared war on Serbia. He wondered how this would affect the Serbian men working in the mills in Gary. Stevo was sure that many of them would go home to fight the Austrians.

Stevo left Dalmacia as a 14-year-old boy with his father. He remembered so many Croatian and Serbian friends there. He couldn't help but wonder if the war would spread throughout Yugoslavia and perhaps further.

The news of the war on Serbia disturbed Stevo. Needing a change, for the first time in the five days aboard the *Princess*, he went to the lower deck. There he found a table with an empty chair and watched the entertainment. Sipping on a mint julep drink, he could only smile and think how tame this drink was compared to slivovitz.

Stevo found himself enjoying the music of several very young black boys making up the band. One was an accomplished cornet player and singer. The music was lively, jazzy, and had the people on deck tapping their feet and hands in time to the music. This was the music Stevo heard and enjoyed in New Orleans. The music played in street parades and funerals. Back then, there were even times he joined in some of these parades, feeling the freedom and pleasure of dancing in the street.

He ordered another mint julep. He looked up at the bright moon and the sparkling stars. The music, the night, the moon all made Stevo feel different. He felt his life was changing more. He no longer felt like the Stevo Markovich of Gary, Indiana.

When the musicians were between songs, Stevo did what he did for the tamburashi at Milan's tavern. He walked up to the cornet player, a thin, young man with a huge white-toothed smile. "I like your music." he said, as he slipped money into the performer's shirt pocket. "What's your name?" Stevo asked.

"Louis." the man answered.

On the sixth and seventh day of the trip, Stevo did walk about both the upper and lower decks and spoke with several fellow passengers. He found himself smiling and not avoiding conversation. He would, however, move on when the conversation started to become personal. He couldn't say what his business was for he no longer was in business. When asked where he was going, he just replied, "To visit family."

He still ate alone in his cabin. On the seventh night he had frog legs, fried potatoes and some rhubarb pie for desert. After his meal he placed a chair outside the door to his cabin. He smoked a cigarette and enjoyed the pleasant night air. The sound of the boat paddles hitting the water and in the distance the eerie haunting call of a loon made the night seem unreal.

The music from the lower deck made its way to where he sat. The sound was softer, but still with a jazz beat to it. Stevo got up once to see who was singing. It was the man he tipped, Louis.

A young man and a woman walked past his chair, nodded, saying "Good evening", then moving on. He was aware that these people were from the south. Their words were soft and melodious as they spoke, not hard as in the North. Stevo saw the couple when they had moved further away from him for privacy, but the bright moon was a spotlight on them as they kissed.

Stevo closed his cabin door and walked around the boat. In the darkness, the lights from the shore glistened like signals. He saw small rowboats with men fishing with lanterns on the boats. In the distance he saw what looked like campfires dotting the shoreline.

The boat would reach New Orleans in the morning. Back in his cabin, Stevo laid out the clothes he would wear for the departure. He neatly stacked the newspapers and books he had read on a table. Under a glass, he left money for his young and efficient porter.

The music from below was not so jazzy or fast at this late hour. Now it was smooth and soft, lulling Stevo into sleep.

His father came to him again in his dreams.

CHAPTER 23

It was close to noon when Stevo disembarked the *Princess*. While waiting for a taxi, he smiled to himself when he noticed that the couple he saw kissing on deck in the moonlight passed one another as if they were strangers. The man was greeted on the dock with a kiss from a pretty woman holding a baby in her arms. Stevo didn't see who greeted the kissing partner of the night before.

The taxi Stevo hired had an extended wire wagon-like cage on its rear. Here the trunks, luggage, and whatever else were loaded, while the passenger rode in the seat behind the driver.

The taxi went to Decatur Street until reaching Canal Street, where it turned north.

Stevo inhaled deeply. He had not realized how much he missed the scent of flowers. The flowers at funerals or weddings in Gary did not overwhelm the senses the way the gardens of New Orleans could.

The taxi stopped to wait for a street parade crossing Canal Street at Bourbon Street. Stevo got out of the taxi to watch the parade of dancers and musicians strutting and dancing in time to the music.

When the parade passed, the taxi continued on with Stevo now wondering how his arrival would be received.

Would his stepmother slam the door in his face? How old would his half brothers, Pietro and Antonio, be now...mid-twenties? What if they didn't want to see him? Surely his stepmother knew he took the hidden Cheroots cigar box filled with money.

Stevo felt his heartbeat quicken as he recognized the block where he had lived from the age of 14 to 24. It still looked the same. Cobblestone street, iron balconies crowded with pots of colorful flowers, and on some, pillows draped on the railing, to air in the sunlight.

Following Stevo's instructions, the taxi pulled into the entrance of the courtyard. In the center of the yard was a tall, bubbling cement water fountain encircled with bushes of fragrant azalea bushes.

There were only two houses within this courtyard. Almost mirror images. Facing the fountain, the house Stevo had lived in was on the left and across the cobblestone pavement was an almost identical house on the right.

When the luggage was unloaded and the taxi paid for, Stevo went to the lower door of the house that was once his home. To the side was a stairway leading to the second floor. Before he knocked, he noticed the windows were not very clean. The brass knocker on the door was not highly polished as he remembered it.

He knocked. Hearing no movement, he knocked again, this time a bit more forcefully. Becoming impatient, he took the stairs to the second floor entrance. It was the same. The house appeared unlived in…deserted. Wondering what to do, he descended the stairs. Going down, he noticed colored red sand on the steps with some gold sparkles mixed in. *What is all that about?* He wondered.

He pulled on the door at the lower lever, hoping by some chance it would open. It did not. He walked to the entrance of the courtyard to Canal Street and looked up at the balcony of the house and saw no blooming plants or a chair.

Back at the door, he looked around. He saw more of that red sand in front of the door. A large clay planter stood to his left with dried, dead flowers in it. Stevo looked at the pot. *Could it still be there? After all these years could it be there?*

He reached behind the pot, feeling the ground. He felt nothing. With both hands he twisted the large planter moving it a little. With a sense of relief, he spotted the key. It had always been there, but seldom used, because his stepmother saw to it that she was always home when Stevo and his father came home from their day working on the river.

It took two tries to get the key to work. The lock behaved as if it didn't recognize the key, but with some hard twisting, Stevo got it open on the second try.

Stevo was assaulted by the smell of stale air. Dust was everywhere.

Where were his stepmother and stepbrothers?

Stevo dragged the trunk and other luggage into the entry which led to the kitchen on the lower level.

The silence, the dust on everything, as well as the dust floating in the air, gave Stevo an eerie feeling. He had prepared himself for a major argument from his stepmother, but perhaps this was worse. What would he find upstairs?

He opened a kitchen window before taking the inside stairs to the second floor.

Once at the upstairs hallway, he was overcome by the stale air. He went into the sitting room and headed immediately for the balcony doors. He turned the latch, pulling both doors open wide. Stevo stepped out on the balcony and breathed in the fresh air.

The words, *Where are they? Where is everyone?* kept running through his mind.

He removed his suit coat and draped it on the balcony rail, not wanting to set it down in the dusty house. Off of the sitting room had been his father and Theresa's bedroom, the master bedroom. Stevo opened a window in this room also.

Stevo hurried down the hallway to the two bedrooms where he had slept and the twins shared the other. He unlatched the windows, flinging them open. The house needed air!

It didn't take long for Stevo to come to the conclusion that the house had been unlived in for quite a while. There was no point in looking for any food or something to drink.

He escaped to the balcony after putting a small metal table and a metal chair there. He draped his suit coat on the back of the chair. Stevo sat in the chair, lit a cigarette and wondered who could tell him what had happened to his stepfamily. For a while he just leaned back in the chair and smoked. Finished with his cigarette, he snuffed it out in the pot of dead leaves next to the table. Standing, he leaned forward onto the balcony rail and surveyed the street below. Black women in brightly-colored skirts and aprons, their hair tied in a kerchief, carried baskets of goods to sell. He heard their songs, "Get your ripe berries here." Or, "I have good pralines, the best in New Orleans." Some women sold flowers from large baskets dangling on their arms. Carriages, taxis and carts pushed by men added to the street sounds.

Most of the people, men, women, and children of various colors passed below the balcony and the sidewalks on both sides of the street.

Across the street, one man stood looking up to where Stevo was leaning on the balcony rail. He caught Stevo's attention.

Stevo wondered if the man was someone he knew or should remember. Instead of a suit, the bearded, long-haired man wore a blue cotton kimono-type garment over his black shirt and black trousers. Instead of a tie, he wore what looked to Stevo like a medallion. He wore no hat and in his hand held a gold knobbed walking stick. Stevo wondered if the walking stick held a hidden blade.

The man looked at Stevo for what seemed a long while. Feeling uncomfortable, Stevo pulled the balcony doors behind him, not closing them completely as he returned to the sitting room.

Since there was no food or anything to drink in the house, he put on his suit coat, but not until he ran a comb through his hair and mustache. Taking a towel, he wiped the dusty mirror and appraised his reflection. *Not bad*, he thought. He placed his pocket watch and chain in the pockets of his vest and looked for his derby hat.

The open kitchen window was low enough for someone to use as an entry, so Stevo closed and latched it before exiting the house. Instead of putting the key back under the planter, he attached it to his watch chain.

Before leaving the courtyard, he glanced around, still not seeing anyone. He thought of going to the other house in the court yard, but it was dark, also looking deserted. He remembered his stepmother, Theresa, telling him to stay away from that house. The house across from his had a lovely patio set up for dining with outdoor furniture and many pots of flowering trees and plants.

He walked out onto the street, looking in the direction where the long-haired man with the walking stick had stood staring up at him. The man was no longer there.

Inside the courtyard, two women, hidden by the shadows, watched as Stevo walked onto Canal Street.

One of the women whispered to the other, "I told you the red sand would bring him back."

Stevo thoroughly enjoyed walking down the street, brushing shoulders with people who smiled and nodded as they passed by. The tiny shops were still open, not closing at a fixed time, for the streets of New Orleans had people of all colors and nationalities walking about at all hours.

One store window caught Stevo's eyes. He noticed different colored sand in each individual bowl displayed in the window. Also he noticed six inch red candles portraying a nude woman or nude man. He remembered that the red candles were meant to bring love, if a piece of cloth, a strand of hair or anything belonging to the one whose love was wanted, was pressed into the wax. The same worked for the black candles, but these candles were meant to bring unhappiness or worse.

He entered the shop and was overwhelmed by the odors of oils and incense. There were bones from assorted animals and what appeared to be bowls of animal teeth.

Hanging on a wire at one wall of the room were bundles of dried herbs or flowers, similar to what Katya and Cleona had drying on their porch back in Gary.

A woman quietly came from behind a curtained doorway. She was tan skinned, her eyes almost black. On her head was a silk red and gold scarf draped like a veil, matching her loose red dress with gold trim at the ends of her wide sleeves.

She startled Stevo when she asked, "Is there something Monseiur wants?"

Just for a moment, Stevo was transported to his youth when he saw such exotic looking women. He remembered his superstitious stepmother telling him, "Don't let them look into your eyes. Look away! They can put a spell on you with their eyes."

Remembering this foolish superstition, Stevo smiled at the woman and asked, "What are the colored sands in the window used for?"

The woman, ever so slightly, brushed past Stevo, making him aware of her the exotic scent she wore. At the window, she asked, "Which color interested you?"

"I just wondered what the red sand was meant to do." he said.

"It brings the person whose name is said when the sand is sprinkled." said the exotic woman. She started to reach into the window, but Stevo stopped her saying, "I didn't want to buy the sand, I was just curious."

He was aware that she was staring at him. Starting to feel uncomfortable, he asked, "What do you have that brings a sense of peace to a house?"

She tilted her head, eyeing him, studying him, as if she could see inside of him. She walked behind a counter and pulled out a box of six-inch light blue tapered candles.

"These will bring peace and happiness to your home." she said.

Stevo took the candles from her hand. He felt an odd sensation as her fingers touched his.

"What do I owe you?" he asked.

She looked deep into his eyes, "Whatever they are worth to you."

CHAPTER 24

Stevo slipped the tissue-wrapped candles in his suit pocket. Smiling at the shop lady, he left to find a place to eat.

Music spilled onto the street from various businesses. He didn't recognize many of the stores. Walking casually, enjoying the sounds and the looks and manners of the people he passed, Stevo was content. Even with the nagging worry of what happened to his family, he felt he belonged on the streets of New Orleans.

He paused at a large, open-gated dining place. One could eat indoors or out. The tables he saw out in the courtyard were covered in white cloths, already set with plates and flatware. Each table had a colorful, low bowl of flowers in the center. Stevo saw bird cages standing at various places in the yard housing parrots of bright colors.

While he was looking at the yard, a waiter approached him, "Will you be dining alone?" he asked.

As if the decision had already been made for him by the waiter, Stevo allowed himself to be escorted to a table away from the entrance. He was pleased to see so many nicely dressed people. The snippets of conversations he heard were a mixture of English, French and Creole. Stevo couldn't see any musicians, but he heard pleasant background music.

The waiter removed the unnecessary place settings, leaving only what Stevo would need. Handing to Stevo a menu with a red tassel tied to the bottom of the center crease, the waiter poured water into a glass in which was a slice of fresh lemon.

Before the waiter could ask what Stevo wanted to drink before ordering, Stevo said, "I will have the alligator steak."

"A good choice." said the waiter asking about a salad, vegetable and more.

Sipping his wine and smoking a cigarette while waiting for his meal, he glanced about the outdoor restaurant. If the food and service was good, Stevo was sure he would return.

His eyes fixed on a figure at the entrance of the courtyard dining area. Standing at the outside of the gate, he again saw the man who had been looking at him from the other side of the street when Stevo was on the balcony.

Stevo caught the attention of a passing waiter asking, "Who is that man at the entrance?"

When the waiter looked in that direction, the bearded man with the walking stick was gone.

After an enjoyable meal, surrounded by music and true New Orleans atmosphere, Stevo paid the check, promising himself to return.

His walk home was a leisurely stroll, stopping to look into store windows or to listen to a sidewalk musician, sometimes accompanied with a young dancer. Stevo always threw a coin in the tip basket or hat on the walkway.

Arriving at the entry to his courtyard, he noticed a lit candle in a round bowl on his neighbor's patio table. Glancing in that direction, he saw a woman at the table. He politely tipped his hat in her direction and proceeded to his own doorway.

"Is that you, Mr. Steve?" the woman called. "If you are Mr. Steve, please join me."

Stevo stopped, more than a little curious and surprised. He removed his hat, turned, and walked to the table, where he saw an older, but obviously once great, beauty sitting in a wicker wheelchair.

"I recognize you, Mr. Steve." she said. "You are the young man who left here some time ago." She motioned to an empty chair at the table, "Please sit."

Stevo sat in the chair, placing his hat on the table. He studied the woman for a moment before saying, "Of course, you are Miss Kara."

Smiling at him, she said in her soft southern drawl, "How kind of you to remember." She was studying his handsome face, making him feel just a bit uncomfortable. She said, "I know by law that absinthe is forbidden, but I do have some bottles of it. May I offer you a glass?"

He smiled broadly saying, "The last time I had absinth was the night before I left here. I would enjoy some. Thank you."

Miss Kara, with a ring-fingered hand, picked up a small brass bell from the table top and rang it.

Almost instantly, a small, older black woman, her head tied with a three-cornered scarf, knotted at the front of her head said, "Welcome home, Mr. Steve."

Stevo rose from his chair and stood in front of the short woman. He studied her for a moment than broke into a smile saying, "Why, I remember you! You are Angel the housekeeper."

Angel said, "Please, Mr. Steve. Sit down. You have no cause to stand for me."

Miss Kara said, "Angel, bring glasses and absinthe for us."

Before Angel turned to leave she said, "We were hoping you would return."

Stevo looked at Miss Kara. "What did she mean by that? That you were hoping I would return."

Miss Kara dismissed the remark with a wave of her hand saying, "We were hoping the house across the way would not stay empty."

Angel returned with the glasses, placing the bottle of absinthe on the table. She asked, "Should I bring a dish of cheese and fruit?"

"Not for me." said Stevo, I have just finished eating.

Miss Kara said nothing, only nodded agreeing with Stevo.

Dusk had turned to darkness while they sipped the green-colored absinthe, which Stevo enjoyed.

Miss Kara looked at Stevo with some affection. Stevo reminded her of his father who was always polite to her, though Theresa his wife spent most of her years ignoring Miss Kara.

Miss Kara gazed passed Stevo to the house where he grew up.

He asked, "How long has the house been empty and…please tell me what happened to everyone."

Miss Kara moved her hips to make herself more comfortable in the wicker chair. She looked at the house, remembering the past. Her dark eyes watered a bit, but no tears came. A slight breeze gently lifted the curls around her face, while the rest of her long hair was tied in a bun at the back. In the candlelight, her porcelain skin almost glowed.

She put her fingertips in the form of a prayer on her lips as she searched for what to tell Stevo.

"Mr. Steve," she began. "The first thing I remember was about your brother, Pietro. Must have been about 6 years ago, we heard he was killed on the docks in a bar fight." She glanced back at Angel, who sat in rocking chair away from the table, knitting. When Angel didn't look up, Miss Kara continued, "When your stepmomma got the news, we heard her screams and then her crying and wailing for days. There was no funeral, because they never found his body."

"Then more than four years ago…" before she could go on, she and Stevo heard Angel get up and leave abruptly.

Miss Kara cleared her throat and continued, "Then more than four years ago, the other boy, Antonio…just up and disappeared."

Stevo said nothing, just looked at Miss Kara. He thought he saw a tear trickle down her cheek.

"Are you alright?" he asked.

She forced a smile. "Forgive me, Mr. Steve. It appears I am an old woman moved by memories." She motioned to the absinth bottle, "Please pour me a little more and for yourself."

Neither of them spoke for a while, thinking about what was said.

Stevo was the first to speak, "What about Theresa? What happened to her?"

"With both her boys gone, she went mad." said Miss Kara. "She would stand up at the bedroom window and curse me and God."

Surprised, Stevo asked, "Why you?"

Miss Kara turned away, shrugging her shoulders, saying, "Who knows?"

The servant, Angel, who was listening at the door of the house, reappeared. She said, "That Theresa never left the house. We knew she didn't have any food. I took food to her. Sometimes she would eat, but mostly she ignored what I left for her." Angel looked at Miss Kara, wondering if she should go on. Miss Kara nodded that she could, so Angel said, "Theresa didn't clean the house or herself. She never went on the balcony or came outside. Then one morning about two years ago, when I went to take her some coffee and toast…I found her dead on her bedroom floor."

With all this information, Stevo was quiet. After a while he asked, "Who took care of the funeral arrangements for Theresa?"

Miss Kara said, "I called Mr. Brouchard at the New Orleans National Bank. We knew that at one time Theresa did her banking there. We were hoping Mr. Brouchard would know what to do."

"Did he take care of the details?" asked Stevo.

"Yes." said Miss Kara. "I couldn't go to the funeral. I guess no one did. Mr. Brouchard told me that he was there and saw to it that it was done properly."

Stevo showed his pack of cigarettes to Miss Kara, his way of asking permission to smoke.

She said, "I'd like one, too please."

They both took drags from their cigarettes and both looked out at Stevo's deserted house. He said, "I was never very fond of Teresa, but it is sad that when she died no one was with her…or even cared."

Miss Kara made no reply. After a few moments she said, "I know your house needs cleaning. Have you made any plans for that?"

"I haven't had time to think about it." Stevo said.

Angel rose from her rocker and came to stand next to where Stevo sat. She said, "I know there is no food. In the morning, when you open the bedroom curtain, I will bring you some coffee and breakfast."

Pleased, Stevo gave Angel a warm smile, "Thank you, Angel. That is very kind of you."

Miss Kara said, "You will need the house cleaned up. If you would like, I can arrange for two reliable women to come tomorrow and get that done for you." Then as an afterthought she asked, "Would you be wanting a regular housekeeper, maybe one that lives in and does the cleaning and cooking?"

Almost with relief, Stevo said, "Miss Kara that would be wonderful. I hadn't thought that far. Thank you."

He noticed that Miss Kara was looking a bit tired, so he said, "Miss Kara, thank you for the pleasure of your company and telling me about my family." He took her hand and kissed it saying, "Thank you for going to the trouble of arranging my household help."

Later, up in the master bedroom, with the lights out, he looked from the window at Miss Kara's patio. The ladies had gone in and the candle on the table no longer burned.

From far in his past, he remembered that his stepmother had called Miss Kara an Octoroon. She had said it as if it were something bad.

Stevo took a cigarette from his almost empty pack, and lit it while looking at the house across the courtyard. He was trying to remember what his father had told him when Stevo asked about Teresa calling Miss Kara an Octoroon.

His father had said that only in New Orleans did the wealthy Creole men take a woman who looked every bit a white woman, but was one-eighth black, provide her with a home and provide an education for any offspring they might have. However the man never married the Octoroon. The men did not live in the house with the woman, though sometimes, it was pretended that the woman was a housekeeper.

Stevo remembered while he was living there, seeing a fancy carriage arrive often in the courtyard. It appeared to always be the same carriage and the same man who went into Miss Kara's house. The carriage would leave coming back later for the man. Once, Stevo saw only the man's profile, but never the full face.

Stevo recalled his father saying, "Theresa has called Miss Kara a whore. That isn't true. She is a lady and I want you to be polite to Miss Kara when you see her."

CHAPTER 25

When Stevo awoke the following morning, he reached for his pocket watch. It was 8:30. He rubbed his eyes, scratched his head, stood up, and stretched. It then occurred to him that he had a good night's sleep. No dreams! For the first time in almost a month his father didn't come to him in his dreams. In fact, he wondered if he had dreamt at all.

Stevo picked up his pocket watch, winding it for the day. He went to the window and drew back the curtains, remembering that Angel would bring him breakfast. He poured water from the pitcher into the wash bowl and washed his face. His dark blue robe with grey piping on the sleeves was on the bed. He put on the robe, slipped his feet into his slippers and went down to the kitchen to unlock the door for Angel.

Back upstairs in the sitting room, he opened the balcony doors wide. The house didn't smell quite as musty as the day before or perhaps he was getting used to it. He stepped out onto the balcony to take in the morning activity on the street.

"Mr. Steve...Mr. Steve, I have your breakfast." called Angel from below. "Where will you eat? I can clean the kitchen table for you."

He was down stairs before she could put down the tray. Stevo said, "I think I want to eat in the sitting room. I will use the desk as a table." He took the tray from the little woman, who smiled at him. "Sure am glad you came home." she said.

Stevo took the tray up to the sitting room, where he placed it on the French desk.

The tray held a coffee pot, a dish covered with a silver lid, silverware, cream and sugar bowls, and a nice white napkin.

He poured himself a cup of coffee and smiled when he smelled the chicory coffee. Now he was home. He had not had chicory coffee since the day he left New Orleans.

When he lifted the lid from the plate, instead of palechinke or warm bread with sugar and cinnamon, he saw fried shrimp stuffed with ham. He almost howled with laughter. This was not a breakfast Ignatz would have prepared.

With his breakfast finished, he poured himself another cup of coffee. He put the tray on a straight backed chair to clear the desktop. With only the coffee cup on the desk, he opened the center drawer of the desk. He saw notes and receipts that meant nothing to him.

There were two deep side drawers which he opened and thumbed through. He found the receipt for his father's burial. It made him stop. He studied it and remembered the guilt he had felt for not helping his father do a roofing job for a friend. It was a fall from the roof that killed his father. A pain he hadn't felt since his father's funeral now gripped Stevo. He remembered how Theresa wanted Stevo to leave, saying the house was hers, left to her by her father. When Stevo asked her what his father had left him, she laughed and told him there was nothing for him.

That memory made Stevo look at the picture on the wall, hiding the opening where he had found and took the Cheroot Cigar box with money in it.

Taking another sip from the coffee cup, Stevo left the desk and went to the picture on the wall. He pushed it aside, remembering how he felt the night he stole the box.

There was still a hole in the plaster, this time, a cardboard box resting on sheets of paper which looked like documents.

Stevo pulled everything out and placed the contents on the desk.

He moved the coffee cup, so as not to spill any on the papers. The first place he looked was in the cardboard box. Just a few bills of paper money were in it. Theresa no longer had Stevo's father's salary to hide.

There were a few loan papers, paid off and marked as such. He picked up a loan document that had his father's name on it. It was for a loan to repair the roof.

Stevo placed his hand on his forehead, as if he were thinking or tying to understand what he was reading. It was the deed to the house…in his father's name! That bitch Theresa told him the house was left to her by her father and that Stevo had no claim to anything!

His hands were shaking. If Theresa were alive, Stevo thought he could possibly strangle her! He went to the balcony, taking in deep breaths of fresh air. He was almost lightheaded. He sat in the metal chair on the balcony and reached into his robe pocket for a cigarette.

Stevo became calm as he smoked. He had planned to go to a bank about having his account transferred from the Gary State Bank to one in New Orleans.

The name on the deed was the New Orleans National Bank. That was the bank he would go to.

While he dressed, he heard the cleaning women downstairs. They called to him letting him know they were there.

He put what money he had brought from Gary into his valise, along with all the papers he found in the secret hole behind the picture.

In the kitchen were two black women, one a bit older and taller than the other.

"The older one said, "I am Serafine, but everyone just calls me Sera." She pointed to the younger woman. "This is

Virgine." Both women wore long skirts with full aprons and their hair covered with the usual three cornered knotted scarf.

Stevo asked, "Which of you is going to live in?"

The younger one named Virgine said, "I am."

Stevo took the house key off of the watch chain and handed it to her. "Have another key made so we each will have one." He handed her some money and left for the bank.

Leaving the courtyard, Stevo glanced over to Miss Kara's patio. Her back was to him so she didn't see him. With her was a beautiful little girl. Stevo guessed she might have been about four years old.

At the bank, Stevo asked to open an account and speak with someone to set up his account to receive money from up north. He was escorted to a desk that was enclosed with a wooden fence-like rail. It had a small gate, which was meant to show this was a private though open area.

Stevo introduced himself to one of the bank managers, a young Mr. Lafon, who was slender, well groomed, and looking every inch a banker in a dark blue suit, white shirt with thin blue stripes, and a blue and maroon necktie.

Offering Stevo a chair, the young Mr. Lafon sat at his desk waiting for Stevo to explain what he wanted in the way of banking.

When Mr. Lafon saw how much Stevo was depositing in both a checking and savings account, the young man was impressed and very attentive to whatever Stevo might want. Forms were filled out and information about the Gary State Bank was provided when Mr. Lafon was informed that money transfers should be coming monthly from Gary.

Mr. Lafon, so very pleased with this impressive new account said, "Can we do anything more for you, Mr. Markovich?"

Before Stevo could mention the papers he found in the house, Mr. Lafon stood up as if to attention. An older, white-haired man opened the entry gate to look at Stevo.

The man said, "Did I hear your name correctly? Are you Mr. Markovich?"

Wondering what this man wanted, Stevo politely rose replying, "Yes, my name is Steve Markovich."

The white-haired man asked, "Was your father Stevo Markovich, the fisherman?"

Now thoroughly confused, Stevo said, "Yes, that was my father."

The white-haired man said to the still standing bank manager, "Thank you, Mr. Lafon. Mr. Markovich and I have some business to attend to."

"Come this way, my boy." said the man, taking Stevo by the elbow and leading him to a private office. On the door were the words: HAROLD BROUCHARD, BANK PRESIDENT.

Stevo recalled that the man Miss Kara called when Teresa had died was Mr. Brouchard from the bank.

"Sit down. We have a lot to talk about." said Mr. Brouchard.

"Excuse me." said Stevo. "How do you know what I came here to talk about?"

Mr. Brouchard offered a box of cigars to Stevo. When Stevo said, "I prefer cigarettes." He was offered a silver box which held cigarettes.

Mr. Brouchard, impeccably dressed all in brown, offered Stevo a light and then lit his cigar. The two men sat a moment puffing on their smokes, when the bank president said, "Tell me what you want to talk about."

From his valise, Stevo pulled out the deed to the house. Showing it to Mr. Brouchard, he said, "When my father died, my stepmother Theresa told me the house was hers, left to her by her father. She informed me that my father had no money left for me." Stevo hesitated before saying, "And...she asked me to leave."

Mr. Brouchard studied Stevo for a while before saying, "I knew the house was in your father's name." He puffed on his cigar and leaned forward in his chair. "I knew all about Theresa. I knew how greedy she was. She had a savings account in her own name. When your father came in to draw some money out, I had to tell him that the savings account was only in Theresa's name."

Mr. Brouchard rose from the desk and went to a small safe behind the desk. "That was when your father and I became good friends." He worked the dials on the safe and pulled out a small brown bank pass book, handing it to Stevo.

Stevo looked at the black ink names written on the cover: Stevo Markovich, Sr. & Stevo Markovich Jr.

Stevo looked up at Mr. Brouchard. "What is this?"

"Open it, my boy." he said, "Look inside."

Stevo was astounded. His father had faithfully, according to the entries, made a small deposit every week for years.

Stevo said, "I don't see any withdrawals."

Back in his chair, Mr. Brouchard said, "That money was meant for you. He never took a cent out once he deposited it."

Placing his elbows on the desk, Mr. Brouchard said, "It is wrong to speak ill of the dead, but I must tell you that I did not like your stepmother." He looked at Stevo for a reaction, seeing none he went on, "She was a rude and greedy woman. When your father was buried and you were gone, she came into the bank with the deed to the house. Demanding that we have it changed making her the owner of the house. I lied and told her we had to wait many years, because you might come back and you would be the rightful heir. She argued with me that her boys were also heirs."

"My boy…" at this Stevo had to stifle a smile. Being referred to as boy amused him. Stevo would soon be 35 years old.

"My boy…" said Mr. Brouchard, "Your father was a gentleman. I especially appreciated that he was kind to your neighbor Miss Kara."

Stevo said, "Miss Kara and I visited last evening. I found her charming. Angel brought me breakfast this morning and arranged for cleaning women."

"Did you meet the little girl?" asked Mr. Bouchard.

"No," said Stevo, "but I think I saw her on the patio when I was leaving to come here."

The old banker shook his head, as if dismissing something he was about to say. Instead he said, "I have more to show you. You may be very pleased."

With a puzzled look, Stevo took the sheets of columned papers Mr. Brouchard offered him. Glancing at them and not understanding, Stevo asked, "What are these papers? What do they mean?"

With a satisfied smile, Mr. Brouchard said, "They mean you are a wealthy young man."

The words were not sinking in. Stevo, looking bewildered, asked, "How can that be?"

Stevo reached for his cigarette resting in the ashtray. He took a deep drag and asked, "Tell me how this is possible."

"My boy, your father did me a great favor looking out for Miss Kara. He was an honorable man, never speaking about my visits to Miss Kara."

Stevo said nothing, remembering the carriage visits into the courtyard those many years ago.

"I held an insurance policy your father gave me. It listed only you as the beneficiary. I want you to sign that policy over to me today."

Dumbfounded, Stevo said, "I don't understand."

Mr. Brouchard rose and started walking back and forth behind his desk, sunlight through the window glistening on his white hair. He said, "I couldn't cash the policy, but I took two hundred dollars of the banks money against it."

Stevo realized he was staring open-mouthed at the banker.

"In my own mind, I wanted to help my old friend and his son, that being you, my boy." Taking a puff on his cigar, Mr. Brouchard, went on with his story, "To be as honest as I could, when I invested my own money, in what I thought was something good, I also invested part of the two hundred dollars. I always invested in the same things, so that if the investment lost your father's money, mine did also."

Stevo said, "I know nothing about investing. All I know is what I learned operating my furniture store."

"Look at the top sheet. I started buying cotton at ten cents a pound in 1906 and then selling it for a profit. Over the years, I have invested my money along with yours in Haitian sugar and coffee futures. We didn't always make money, but in the long run, we have done very well."

Stevo looked at the figures on the sheet. He asked, "Do you mean thcse figures are how much money I have in this bank?"

"It is all yours once you sign the insurance form over to the bank for the two hundred dollars I took as seed money."

Stevo took the pen Mr. Brouchard offered him. "Is this where I sign?" he asked.

Mr. Brouchard nodded. Stevo handed him the signed document and said, "I am almost speechless. Should the bank take a commission for these transactions?"

With a gentle knock on the glass enclosed wall with his ring finger, Mr. Brouchard summoned his secretary. He handed her a stack of papers saying, "Make copies of all of these for Mr. Markovich."

When the secretary exited the room, Mr. Brouchard said, "You can cash it all in, or I can continue as I have been, investing a little at a time."

"I don't know what to say." said Stevo. "I have money to live on and more should be coming each month from my other bank." Stevo stood up and walked back and forth on his side of the desk. He looked at Mr. Brouchard saying again, "I don't know what to say."

The old banker smiled warmly at Stevo. "I hope we can be as good friends as your father and I were. We didn't mix in the same circles, but we understood and respected each other."

Mr. Brouchard said, "It will take a while to make copies of all the papers. I will have them delivered to your home tomorrow, if that is alright with you."

Stevo rose to leave, extending his hand to Mr. Brouchard. He said, "I think I would like to leave matters as they stand. You have been a marvelous manager of my father's money. I couldn't ask for more."

As Stevo turned to leave, he saw through the glass windows of the office, the mysterious, bearded, long-haired man walking towards the exit doors of the bank.

"Do you know that man?" Stevo pointed his valise in the bearded man's direction.

"Almost everyone knows Michael Dukane. He is a very famous portrait painter in New Orleans."

CHAPTER 26

The next morning, Stevo, dressed in his robe, opened the bedroom door to find a spotlessly clean, fresh-smelling sitting room. The balcony doors were already opened to bring in the sweet morning air. He noticed that on a side table burned one of the blue candles he purchased earlier, covered with a protective glass chimney.

On the desk was a tray with a silver pot of coffee and in the covered plate Stevo found sugared beignets. He was delighted with the New Orleans form of square donuts. He preferred these to the heavy breakfast of fried shrimp stuffed with ham Angel brought the morning before.

Hearing the street sounds, he gathered his tray and carried it to the balcony table. He poured himself a cup of the chicory coffee, savoring the smell of it.

Stevo stood on the balcony and looked at the passing street vendors. A woman carried a basket on her head, heaped with colorful blossoms. He called down to her, "How much are your flowers?"

She held up one finger for one dollar, saying "For a bunch."

"How much for the whole basket of flowers?" asked Stevo.

The woman removed the basket from her head and set it on the cobblestone walkway. Looking up at Stevo with surprise, she said, "I have to count them."

"Stay there." Stevo called down. When he returned, he threw to her a ten dollar gold coin.

The startled woman caught the coin and her black face broke into a huge grin.

"I'll bring these up to you." she said.

"Not to me." said Stevo. "Take them all to the other house in the courtyard."

He went to the bedroom and opened the curtain so he could see Miss Kara's house across the way. Stevo watched as the flower seller went to the patio door. After a moment, he saw Angel open the door. He saw some conversation and the flower seller turn towards his house and pointed to it. Angel stepped out onto the patio and saw him in the window. She gave him a big smile and a wave.

Back on his iron balcony, he sipped his coffee, and ate a beignet before lighting a cigarette. He missed his usual assortment of newspapers. Just as he was deciding to pick some up when he left the house that morning, he noticed a young boy selling papers on the corner. Stevo gave a sharp whistle to get the boy's attention.

The young boy came running under the balcony.

Stevo found a liberty head nickel in his pocket and tossed it to the boy, who in turn rolled up the paper and made a good toss up to the balcony.

Stevo called down to the boy, "If I am not here when you come with the papers, go to my door and the housekeeper will pay you. Bring one each day."

Pleased, the boy smiled and waved to Stevo as he went on his way.

Stevo, done with his beignets, took his coffee cup into the sitting room. He poured himself more coffee then spread the newspaper on the desk to read it.

After reading the paper, Stevo went into the bedroom and dressed, choosing the lightest weight suit he had because of the heat. He decided to go hatless today.

Coming out of the bedroom, he saw Virgine gathering up the breakfast tray.

"Good morning, Mr. Steve." she said.

"Good morning, Virgine. I enjoyed the beignets. It has been over ten years since I have had any." Then he added, "By the way," he reached into his trouser pocket, "you will need household money." He handed her several silver certificates. "Just keep track of what you spend so I will know what food and supplies for the house cost." As he descended the stairs he called up to her, "You don't have to ask me every time you need to purchase something."

Outside, Stevo looked over to Miss Kara's patio. The pretty little girl, with light brown banana curls framing her face, dressed in a pink pinafore, sat alone at the table. She didn't see Stevo, so he kept walking onto the street.

On the street, it wasn't long before he saw an empty carriage. He hailed it and told the driver, "St. Anne's Catholic Church."

The church had been built in the mid 1800's. It was where Stevo, his father, and Theresa went each Sunday, and later with the twins. The last time Stevo had been in this beautiful church was for his father's funeral.

He paid the carriage driver, not wanting him to wait while Stevo went into the church. The building was beautiful with an arched entry above two wooden doors, sporting colored red and yellow glass inserts.

Once inside, Stevo was moved by the beauty of the interior. The Stations of the Cross done in gold leaf were on the walls. In niches, were hand-carved marble statues of various saints.

Stevo dipped his fingers in the holy water font, made the sign of the cross and genuflected. He slipped into the last pew, knelt down, and bowed his head. He was overcome with emotion. When he was in the Slovak Church in Whiting, for Mato and Marjan's weddings, he did not feel moved as he was now.

After a while, he looked to the front of the church at the altar. The communion rail, where he had knelt to receive the blessed host, and the confessional in the center of the church against the south wall, were all as he remembered.

There were a few people scattered in the pews, some just sitting, others holding a rosary or a prayer book.

Stevo rose, slipping out of the pew. He walked around the church of his youth looking at everything, feeling as if he were visiting old friends. He stopped at the gold-painted iron stand with vigil lights encased in red glass. Above the stand was a statue of the Virgin Mary, with her hands outstretched. Stevo knelt, said another prayer for his father, then picking up a wick, lit a candle. He paused…lighting two more candles, one for Katya and one for Milan.

At the back of the church, instead of leaving, he sat in the last pew. He thought about several things, such as his Katya dying so young, and Milan being killed in his tavern. But the most pressing thought was that he had not dreamt of his father since coming to New Orleans. Was it possible that his father's spirit wanted Stevo back in New Orleans?

Stevo walked the short distance to the cemetery where his father was interred. Strange, but Stevo couldn't remember where his father's above ground mausoleum was.

He walked among the stone and cement crypts of various sizes and designs. Some had the names carved on the sides or on the doors. For others, there was a burial stone, carved and placed next to the door of the crypt.

Stevo recognized his father's crypt without reading the name. A cross stood above the doorway, while the door had two fish carved into it.

Stevo leaned his forehead against the white outer wall of the crypt. He placed his outstretched hands flat on the wall. He felt at peace for the first time in years. He felt as if his father's spirit was with him.

Later, walking though the open gate of the courtyard of his house, he saw Miss Kara in her wicker wheelchair and the little girl on their patio.

Miss Kara, dressed in a blue and white floral caftan, called out to him, "Thank you for the lovely flowers."

The little girl ran to Stevo with a rose in her hand. She said, "For you."

Stevo knelt down so he could be closer to her size, saying "Well, thank you pretty little lady."

She beamed with pride as he took the rose from her hand.

"What is your name?" he asked.

"Kate. I am Kate." she said.

"Well Kate, thank you for the rose." He said, looking with wonder at the little girl's face. It was as if he knew her, but of course, he couldn't and did not.

He stood, waved to Miss Kara and went into his house, where he found another blue candle burning in the kitchen. This one did not have glass chimney over it.

Upstairs in the sitting room, he noticed what he thought to be the file of copies from the bank. He went into his bedroom, removed his suit coat, undid his stiff collar, and unbuttoned the top two buttons of his white shirt. He rolled his shirt sleeves as he walked back into the sitting room.

On the desk was again a silver tray. This time instead of coffee it held a bottle of Sazerac Brandy. It was pink in color and when Stevo lifted the stopper, he was aware of a slightly medicinal scent. He poured a very small amount in a stemmed cordial glass and took a taste. Surprisingly, it tasted better than he had expected.

Stevo started to open the large, flat brown envelope from the bank, when he noticed there was a smaller, cream-colored envelope addressed with very nice handwriting in black ink to Mr. Steven Markovich.

He pulled open the center drawer of the desk and found a carved Chinese, bone letter opener. Opening the envelope, he withdrew a single sheet of folded paper. It read:

Mr. Brouchard and his sister, Evalynn Spencer, request the honor of your presence at the unveiling of a portrait by Michael Dukane at their home Saturday evening. A small dinner party will be held before the formal presentation of the portrait at seven in the evening.

Stevo stared at the invitation, reading the address. He was bewildered at being invited to the Brouchard home. He recognized the address and knew what type of home he could expect to find there.

He walked into the bedroom and looked over his suits. Did he have the proper clothing for a portrait unveiling? Was the dinner party a formal affair? Most of all, Stevo wondered if this sort of social engagement was out of his league. After all, he was used to eating barbequed lamb and green onions with his fingers; he also ate strudel and nut roll with his fingers.

Stevo didn't bother to put on his collar and tie. He hurried down the stairs, shirt sleeves rolled up and two buttons of his shirt still undone. Stevo was pleased to see Miss Kara, in her wheelchair holding a parasol as she watched Kate playing with a rag doll. Hearing footsteps behind her, Miss Kara turned, saying, "Hello Mr. Steve. What brings you here twice in one day?"

Stevo handed her the invitation, saying, "I don't know what would be the proper dress for such an event. Also, I don't know if I have the proper manners to go to this dinner party."

Kate came close to Stevo, showing him her doll. It was a little, black cloth doll in a long skirt with black yarn hair. She laughed as she showed Stevo that when she flipped the doll over, the long skirt covered the black doll showing that instead of legs, there was a white, blonde yarn-haired doll. Two dolls in one.

Miss Kara said, "Kate, go tell Angel to bring us some cold lemonade."

Kate ran into the house, flipping the skirt up and down, as she skipped into the house, each time revealing the different doll.

Seeing the look on Stevo's face, as Kate disappeared into the house, Miss Kara said, "My granddaughter." With a lump in her throat she said, "Her Momma passed."

After a moment, Miss Kara, holding her parasol to shade her from the sun said, "Of course you have the manners." She took the invitation Stevo offered to her. She visibly frowned when she saw the name Evalynn but said nothing.

Finished with reading the invitation, Miss Kara gave the letter back to Stevo saying, "If this was meant to be a formal event, you would not have received a hand-written note. Instead it would have been done by a printer. As for your clothes, a dark suit would probably be good and a black tie. Do you have a black suit?"

"Yes, I have a rather good black suit." said Stevo, not finding it necessary to tell her he had been a funeral director.

Angel smiled seeing Stevo at the table. She carried a tray, glasses filled with shaved ice, and a pitcher of freshly-made lemonade.

"Hello Mr. Steve." she said. placing the tray on the table. "Thank you for the flowers. There are so many, I even have a bunch in my room."

"You are very welcome." said Stevo watching her fill the glasses. When the glasses were full, she returned to the house.

Miss Kara closed her parasol and leaned it against her chair.

Stevo asked, "Am I supposed to send the hostess flowers with my note of acceptance?"

Miss Kara handed him the glass, saying, "No, you send flowers after the event with your thank you note. It is polite to tell her what a nice evening you had or mention the good meal."

They both sipped the freshly-made lemonade in silence for a while.

Stevo said, "I don't understand why Mr. Brouchard would want to invite me to his home. We don't know each other, except for our meeting at the bank."

Miss Kara looked at Stevo and said, "Perhaps he wants to tell you something."

CHAPTER 27

On Saturday, the day of the dinner party and portrait unveiling, Evalynn Spencer was going over the Picayune Creole Cookbook, reading the recipes to her black cook. The old cook didn't say anything as the recipe was being read to her, after all…she knew how to make filé gumbo!

Evalynn Spencer loved living in her brother's home. She especially liked the role of woman of the house. Her brother, Harold Brouchard, was not married. He already had a woman of mixed races he had been supporting for more than twenty years. It appeared he wouldn't…couldn't marry the woman he loved.

Though Evalynn was grateful to have a home for herself and her seventeen-year-old daughter, Coralynn, she still held some resentment towards her brother.

Evalynn knew her husband drank more than he should have, lost money gambling, and when he took money from the bank…well, Harold should have protected his brother-in-law instead of letting him be fired from his position.

It was not long before most of their New Orleans friends knew of John Spencer's shame and dismissal from the bank. Because of the scandal, Evalynn was not invited to functions as she once was. As a result of his lack of work, her husband frequented the docks, drinking and gambling with money made from whatever he could sell.

When John Spencer was found dead in the room of a mulatto prostitute, Harold Brouchard stopped paying the upkeep on the Spencer house and took his sister and niece into his home.

The Brouchard home was originally built in 1846 on Chartres Street. It had the look of an Italian Villa with Greek columns. The house was built by Brouchard's grandfather for his then bride-to-be.

The house had a ballroom, a large parlor, and a rectangular dining room. The bedrooms were at the back of the house facing the fenced-in garden and fountains.

When Stevo stepped down from the carriage, in front of the iron staircase leading to the entry doors, he hoped he could hide the fisherman's son that was always inside of him. It wasn't yet seven o'clock so Stevo hoped he wasn't too early.

The door was opened by a black servant, who took Stevo's hat and asked his name. Stevo was led to a small side room, where the servant announced his arrival.

Mr. Brouchard left the people he was with and came to Stevo, his hand extended. "My boy, so happy you came. Let me introduce you to everyone."

The first introduction was to his sister, Evalynn Spencer, elegantly dressed in a long, slim green evening dress, which was beautiful with her gray green eyes and her silver hair.

She extended her hand, and made a slight curtsy while Stevo took her hand and made a respectable bow.

Next, he met Coralynn Spencer, Evalynn's daughter. Coralynn, dressed in white with blue silk flowers at the waist, smiled shyly, very impressed with the handsome Steve Markovich.

Another guest was Captain DeMare. Stevo did not know that Capt. DeMare was an extremely wealthy importer from Jamaica making his fortune bringing bananas or plantains to New Orleans on his own ships. The Captain bowed, shaking Stevo's hand, turned to his young companion, dressed in red, saying to Stevo, "Sir, may I introduce, Miss Carla Fontaine, my fiancée."

"Enchanté" said Stevo, remembering his bit of New Orleans French from long ago.

"And here is our guest of honor." Mr. Brouchard turned towards the artist Michael Dukane.

Michael Dukane, dressed always in black trousers and shirt, over which this time, he wore a long, French brocade coat of blue and gold patterns. Again, no tie, instead a large, crystal cross almost four inches in length.

The artist's smile was not warm or friendly, just polite. Dukane said, "I have seen you around town." Stevo replied, "And I have noticed you."

The dining table was beautifully set on a white-on-white patterned cloth. A low, silver bowl of flowers served as the centerpiece. Place cards were at each seat. Mr. Brouchard was at the head of the table with Stevo at his right.

During the meal, Stevo realized he needn't have been so worried. The place settings and service pieces were not overly elaborate. A French wine was served with the gumbo, which was delicious.

The conversation throughout the meal was mostly about the Captain's land in Jamaica, his boats, and the reason for his invitation to dinner which was that if he liked the portrait to be unveiled later, he would commission Dukane to do one of his fiancée.

Carla Fontaine did not speak much throughout the meal. She appeared to be shy, but she did steal glances at Stevo, which did not go unnoticed by Coralynn Spencer. At one point, Mr. Brouchard's niece gave Carla a hard look and the girl blushed, dropping her eyes.

After the table was cleared, the party moved into the parlor for coffee and brandy. The room was plush with large pieces of furniture and the wooden floor glistened like clean glass.

Leaving the dining room, Coralynn took Stevo's arm and stayed near him.

Stevo kept glancing at Dukane, who he found to be mysterious. Every now and then, Dukane would look towards Stevo.

Servants appeared with trays of glasses for brandy and cups for the coffee.

Conversation flowed easily among the guests. Michael Dukane was the center of attention. There was no doubt he was charismatic. He was born into an old, French New Orleans family, studied painting in Europe and at a young age, already acquired fame as a portrait artist.

To his niece, Mr. Brouchard said, "Excuse us my dear." Leaving behind a disappointed Coralynn, Mr. Brouchard took Stevo's elbow, "Let's go out on the terrace. I want to tell you something no one needs to hear."

The garden was beautiful in the moonlight. The sounds of the fountains were pleasant.

Mr. Brouchard pulled a cigar from his coat pocket, saying, "I don't have cigarettes on me."

"I have mine." said Stevo, taking one from an opened pack. He then struck a match and held it for the old banker, before lighting his cigarette.

They stood at the terrace wall, smoking in silence, enjoying the evening air.

Stevo broke the silence asking, "What was it you wanted to tell me?"

Mr. Brouchard blew a puff of cigar smoke into the night air. Looking at Stevo, he said, "My boy, I owe so much to your father, that the small thing I did with the investments does not repay my debt." He looked at Stevo's puzzled reaction to this statement. "You see," he went on, "Your father saved Miss Kara's life and gave us a daughter."

"I don't understand…how is that possible?" asked Stevo, looking intently at the banker.

Mr. Bouchard turned his back to the wall, leaned against it, and looked at Stevo. "You see, Kara was carrying our child." He waved his cigar in the air, "I was at a ball given by one of our wealthy bank depositors. At the same time, Kara's doctor was in the next parish on an emergency."

The old man's face revealed the concern he suffered at the memory of almost losing Miss Kara. He went on with his story, "Angel ran to your home and knocked on the door. Theresa answered. When she heard that Kara was having trouble delivering the baby, instead of coming to help, Theresa slammed the door in Angel's face."

"Oh, dear God." whispered Stevo.

"Angel went back to the house, unable to help Kara, who was crying in pain."

Here, Mr. Brouchard took a deep breath before continuing the story. "Your father came bursting through the door calling for Angel. She heard him and showed him to the bed where Kara lay crying. I don't know how your father did it, but he turned the baby around and out came our Annette." Now the old man had tears in his eyes. "She was not breathing. No matter how much your father struck her backside, she didn't breathe."

"Your father yelled out to Angel, 'Get me some real cold water!' Angel told me how your father kept putting the baby in the cold water and pressing on her little body…over and over again, until she let out a good cry."

Now the old man had tears in his eyes. "You see," he said, "because of your father we had our beautiful Annette for sixteen years…then Kate came. When Kate was born, Annette died."

Stevo stamped out his cigarette on the wall, throwing the butt into the tall flowers nearby. Mr. Brouchard turned again to face the garden, resting his arms on the wall.

He said, "I have more to tell you about Annette."

"There you are!" Mr. Brouchard's sister came onto the terrace, in her hand a lace fan. "We are ready to see the portrait. What have you two been gabbing about out here so long?"

As soon as the two men entered the house, Coralynn joined Stevo, putting her arm through his. In the large parlor, all the guests stood away from the huge canvas on a large wooden easel. The canvas was covered with a white sheet. With a servant on one side and Dukane on the other, they two men lifted the sheet.

There was a moment of brief silence, then the murmurs of approval and a loud continuous applause.

Stevo said to Coralynn, "He caught your beauty in the painting." The comment made Coralynn's face beam and she gave Stevo a beautiful smile.

Filled with pride, Dukane made a slight bow, stepping out of the way for the guests to approach the much-admired oil painting of Coralynn Spencer.

Captain DeMare announced, "Absolutely beautiful. I definitely want you to paint a portrait of my Carla.

When it was Stevo's turn to get a closer view he said, "This is fantastic."

Dukane asked, "Do you know art?"

"Not really." said Stevo, "But for a while we had a Leger and a Braque painting in our store."

Dukane stroked his beard as he looked at Stevo, who continued to study the portrait. He was developing a new respect for Steve Markovich.

CHAPTER 28

In the two weeks after the dinner party at the Brouchard house, Stevo was settling into a routine of sightseeing in New Orleans. While living there as a young boy and later a young man, he hadn't realized what a lovely city New Orleans was.

Every day was an adventure. He shopped in the French Market and more than once found something that made him think...*Katya would love this.* Stevo noticed that he was no longer feeling pain when he thought of Katya. His memories made him feel love, but also some guilt for not feeling the pain he had lived with for several months.

Stevo had been in New Orleans for more than a month. He wrote a letter to Mato, telling him about the house he now owned, but nothing about his family. All the time he was in Gary, he never talked about his family in New Orleans. He definitely didn't write about the money Mr. Brouchard saved for him.

When Stevo wrote to Barbra and Josef, he let them know he hoped they were enjoying being parents and were happy in their home. He mentioned meeting a successful artist and what beautiful portraits he painted.

There was China Town. Stevo thought this may be where Dukane acquired some of the exotic robes he wore instead of a suit coat.

Stevo never tired of walking along the waterfront, listening to fishermen speaking Croatian, along with others speaking Italian, French, Creole, and what Stevo thought to be Jamaican. He stopped in the waterfront bars for a drink, savoring the atmosphere, and remembering that he was once one of these sunburned, strong-bodied men.

In each of the neighborhoods he visited, he heard the music and songs of the people. He could smell their food because many of them had little fires in their courtyards and cooked their meals outdoors.

Still, as much as Stevo enjoyed discovering New Orleans again, he felt useless. He had worked all his life, first as a fisherman, then at his store in Gary. In Gary each day had been filled with activity.

Here, his circle of friends included Miss Kara, Angel, and little Kate. Occasionally Stevo would see Mr. Brouchard when he went to the bank and the two would have lunch at a nearby outdoor restaurant.

When Stevo mentioned that he was becoming bored with nothing useful with which to occupy his time, Mr. Brouchard offered him a job at the bank, which Stevo declined. He could not see himself as a bank clerk or even as a bank manager.

His visits with Miss Kara were short ones. She hadn't been feeling well and often when on the patio, she would be lying on a cot, rather than sitting in her wheelchair. Stevo was concerned about his neighbor, especially when he saw the worried looks on Angel's face.

Stevo received notes from Mr. Brouchard's niece, Coralynn. She sent invitations to various events taking place such as programs or musical events. So far, Stevo managed to find plausible excuses to avoid going with her. He dreaded the day Mr. Brouchard might ask Stevo to start seeing his niece which would mean dating her. That hadn't happened yet.

But, today a note came from Mr. Brouchard asking Stevo to stop by the bank for a financial matter and perhaps lunch.

When Stevo arrived, he saw Coralynn in the bank president's glass-enclosed office. Young and pretty Coralynn smiled brightly at Stevo as he was ushered into the room

Stevo kissed Coralynn's hand and shook hands with Mr. Brouchard.

"I sent for you," said Mr. Brouchard, "to let you know that a transfer came from your Gary bank. It appears to be a payment on the sale of your store."

"That's encouraging." said Stevo. "It means he must be doing alright with the business."

Mr. Brouchard stood and reached for his hat on the coat rack. "Let's go to lunch." he said, "I have an early afternoon appointment."

At an outdoor café only two buildings down from the bank, the trio found a shaded table already set for them. Stevo held the chair for Coralynn who made no effort to hide her admiration for him. Stevo saw it and hoped he did nothing to encourage the girl.

Somewhere between the fried shrimp and sautéed plantain, Mr. Brouchard said, "A young man such as yourself should be thinking of getting married."

Stevo kept his eyes on Mr. Brouchard, avoiding Coralynn, saying, "I am in mourning and have been for several months. You see…after less than a year of marriage to someone I loved greatly, she died."

Mr. Brouchard gave Coralynn a quick glance, but Stevo kept his eyes on the banker. Stevo didn't want to see Coralynn's reaction.

Mr. Brouchard cleared his throat, and took a drink from his water glass before saying, "I am sorry, my boy. You never mentioned you had been married."

Stevo said, "I find it difficult to talk about Katya."

For the rest of the meal, Coralynn never said a word. The table conversation between Mr. Brouchard and Stevo was mainly about the food or banking.

When the dessert of caramel pie was finished, served with strong coffee, Coralynn stood saying, "Uncle Harold, I really must leave." She gave Stevo a weak smile. Kissing her uncle on the cheek, she hurried away from the table.

Stevo, who had been standing, sat down to see a very embarrassed look on Mr. Brouchard's face.

Mr. Brouchard said, "Steve, I am so sorry to have embarrassed you this way." Getting no reaction from Stevo he continued, "You see, Coralynn has taken quite a fancy to you. Had I known you were in mourning…well, this would not have happened."

Stevo pushed his empty dessert plate aside and pulled his coffee closer. Lighting a cigarette he said, "Please don't give it a thought. Coralynn is a lovely girl, just not for me."

Changing the subject, Stevo asked, "How concerned should I be about Miss Kara? She doesn't call me over. She only lies on the lounge in the shade."

Mr. Brouchard looked around. Seeing no one near to hear their conversation, he said with tears welling in his eyes, "Oh my boy…we may lose her."

Stevo reached across the table touching the man's hand, "What do you mean…lose her?"

With his hand, the banker brushed away a tear that escaped down his cheek before saying, "It all started long ago. She wasn't yet in the wheel chair. Kara was younger and stronger the night she tried to fight off your brother Antonio."

Stevo's jaw dropped. It was a few seconds before he could find his voice. "What do you mean fight him off?"

"He saw my carriage arrive and leave in a matter of minutes." said Mr. Brouchard. "He probably thought Kara left with me. Thinking that Angel was alone in the house with Annette, Antonio slipped into the house and found Annette's room."

Stevo was feeling ill, fearing what he would hear next. The tortured look on Mr. Brouchard's face confirmed Stevo's fears. "Kara heard Annette's cries and struggle."

"Oh, Dear God!" said Stevo.

"He must have been drunk, because he ignored Kara when she tried to pull him off Annette." It was obvious to Stevo that telling this story was hard for Mr. Brouchard. It took him a moment to compose himself. He continued, "Kara grabbed a metal lamp from a table top and struck Antonio on the back with it. He pushed Kara to the ground, wrestling the lamp from her hand. She was on her hands and knees when he struck her in middle of her back." He motioned to the waiter, "Some brandy please." Mr. Brouchard looked to Stevo who shook his head indicating he didn't want any.

Neither man spoke for a while. Stevo watched the banker drink the glass of brandy in one swallow.

After a moment, Mr. Brouchard said, "After that night, no one heard or saw Antonio again. That was when Theresa started cursing Kara, blaming Kara for Antonio's disappearance."

"My God!" said Stevo. "I wish I could do something."

"There is something you can do." said Mr. Brouchard sadly. "You can take Kate when Kara is gone."

Stevo stared at the man. "I?" he said, "I know nothing of caring for children."

With great sadness, Mr. Brouchard said, "I can't take my lovely granddaughter to my home, because I don't know how well my sister would take it. She has never approved of my association with Kara, because she is of mixed race."

He motioned to the waiter with his empty brandy glass. Stevo said, "I'll have one now."

Mr. Brouchard said, "You were the only one we could think of who could care for Kate. We didn't know where you were." He sipped his brandy, "Angel even resorted to voodoo to find you. She had what she believed was magic sand sprinkled at your house."

Stevo smiled, but it was a sad smile. He said, "I saw the red sand." Stevo lit a cigarette and took a sip of the brandy before saying, "For a month before I decided to come here, my father came to me in my dreams, almost every night. It was as if he wanted me here."

"My boy," said Mr. Brouchard, pleading with his eyes and voice, "promise me you will stay in New Orleans and take care of my granddaughter…your niece."

Stevo walked slowly back to his home. He had so much to think about. The news about his half-brother disturbed him greatly. That a brother of his could do such an outrageous act sickened him.

Entering the courtyard, Stevo looked over at Miss Kara's patio. He saw her in her new usual place, on the lounge. To his surprise, Michael Dukane was sitting next to her, holding her hand.

Stevo was torn, should he go pay his respects to Miss Kara or should he respect their privacy and not go there? His curiosity got the better of him, *Why was Dukane here?*

Dukane heard Stevo's steps on the cobblestones. Recognizing Stevo, he smiled, saying, "Come sit with us. We have been talking about you."

Stevo went to Miss Kara and knelt next to her lounge. "I have been having lunch with Mr. Brouchard." he said, looking at her very pale face, which seemed to have aged greatly in just a few days.

She lifted her hand and placed it on his cheek. She said, "I am happy you are here." Her hand dropped as if she didn't have the strength to hold it up. Stevo took her hand placing it back on his cheek, holding it there.

As if Dukane was not there. Miss Kara said to Stevo, "What did you and Harold talk about?" Her voice was weak and low.

Stevo was heartsick as he replied, "We talked about you, Annette, little Kate and…and…Antonio."

He put her hand back on her lap. She said, "Then you know it all?"

"Yes." said Stevo, "I know it all."

In a voice so low and weak, Stevo could hardly hear her as she asked, "Did he ask you about Kate?"

With a lump in his throat, Stevo said, "He asked me…and…I said yes."

CHAPTER 29

Both Stevo and Dukane realized that Miss Kara was extremely tired. Together, they lifted her onto her wicker wheel chair and pushed her into the house. Angel directed them to Kara's room where they gently put her on her soft bed. Stevo kissed Miss Kara on the cheek, while Michael Dukane kissed her hand. She was asleep before they were out of the room.

Sitting on the parlor floor was little Kate. Stevo studied her face and realized the reason she had looked familiar to him was that she had his father's eyes.

Seeing the two men, Kate asked, "Is my mémé feeling better?"

Outside in the courtyard, Stevo said, "Come Dukane, I have some Sazerac we can share."

Virgine was in the kitchen peeling potatoes. She rose when she saw them.

"Bring some cordial glasses." said Stevo, showing Dukane the way to the stairs.

Once upstairs, Stevo said, "Take off your coat if you like. Make yourself comfortable." Stevo slipped off his suit coat while Michael Dukane removed his long exotic coat, this one in shades of purple.

Stevo already had the bottle of Sazerac in his hand when Virgine appeared with the tray of glasses.

"Let's sit on the balcony. It is cooler there." said Stevo. Where Virgine found another metal chair to put on the balcony, Stevo didn't know. He only knew the girl was a wonder.

Stevo placed the bottle and glasses on the table. Michael Dukane was already sitting as Stevo poured the pink drink into the glasses.

Stevo sat in his chair and both men lifted their glasses in a toast.

"What shall we drink to?" asked Dukane.

"To Miss Kara," said Stevo. "Later we can drink to our health."

Each man took a sip of the brandy. Stevo offered Dukane a cigarette.

Both men sipped and smoked in silence for a while, when Stevo asked, "Why were you watching me that morning about a month ago when I was standing on this balcony?"

Dukane said, "I have been watching for your brother ever since Kate was born. If he ever does return, I may kill him."

Stevo's eyes grew wide. "Seriously, why do you want to kill him?"

"Because, Annette and I were engaged. We were waiting for my parents to return from their summer in France before we got married."

He finished his drink holding the glass out to Stevo for more.

Dukane said, "Before my parents returned to New Orleans, we discovered Annette was pregnant by Antonio's attack." He sipped his drink, "It didn't matter to me. I would have married her regardless, but she wouldn't marry me saying it would shame my family. I told Mr. Brouchard and Miss Kara that it didn't matter to me, but they said the decision was Annette's."

Dukane stroked his beard as if lost in a memory. After a few moments, he said, "When the doctors could not get Miss Kara to walk from the strike on her back by Antonio, Annette nearly lost her mind. She felt as if she caused it, not Antonio."

Dukane looked at Stevo, "I didn't like your brother before he attacked Annette. After that, I hated him. I was wishing we could still have duels, for I wanted to run a blade through him or shoot him with a pistol."

Stevo refilled their cordial glasses. He said, "And now you dislike me because of Antonio."

"Not anymore." said Dukane. "I grew up in New Orleans and I knew what bad reputations your brothers, excuse me…half-brothers had. Now that I know you, it is as if you weren't part of their family."

"I wish I could say they weren't. I wish I could say someone besides my father was responsible for their birth, but…but, when I looked at Kate's eyes, I saw my father's eyes."

Dukane puffed on his cigarette. He looked at Stevo who was staring out into space. Dukane asked, "Are you considering marrying Coralynn Brouchard?"

Stevo almost choked on his sip of brandy. "Why do you ask that?" he demanded.

"Because, I am close friends with Coralynn and she told me she really liked you." said Dukane.

Stevo said, "The subject of my marrying came up. No mention of Coralynn, of course. But when I said that I was in mourning for my wife, the subject was pretty much closed."

"I am sorry." said Dukane sincerely. "It appears we both carry pain for the loss of someone we loved."

"What did Coralynn's mother think of you being engaged to Annette?" asked Stevo.

"So, you know about her attitude toward mixed races." replied Dukane.

Stevo said, "Mr. Brouchard told me that Mrs. Spencer did not approve of his long relationship with Miss Kara."

"Annette broke off our engagement before anyone but Miss Kara and Mr. Brouchard knew of it. They both approved. Mr. Brouchard was going to speak to my parents hoping there would be no disapproval on their part. But," he sighed, "it never was necessary once Annette refused to marry me because of what happened to her."

Stevo said, "You and Mr. Bouchard seem to be very good friends."

"He has been wonderful." said Dukane. "Because of his help and support, I have become a busy portrait painter. Mr. Brouchard knows all the people who would want a portrait and can afford to pay me well."

"Such as Captain DeMare?" said Stevo.

"Yes." said Dukane. "I painted Coralynn's portrait as a gift, but no one knew that. We planned the unveiling especially for the Captain's visit to his fiancée."

Dukane was starting to feel the effects of several glasses of the Sazerac. He said, "I had better be leaving, before I fall asleep,"

As Dukane was helped with his long embroidered coat, he asked Stevo, "What are your plans, now that you will stay in New Orleans?"

"I am not sure." said Stevo. Once they were in the courtyard, Stevo said, "There is an empty carriage. Let me help you climb in."

Later in the evening, Stevo, in his bathrobe, stood in front of his window in the dark bedroom. He looked out at Miss Kara's house. All he saw was a dim light, probably from the parlor.

He realized he had a lot to think about, and plans to be made for his future in New Orleans, but what would he do? He didn't want to go back on the docks. He didn't want to work in the bank. Maybe conduct funerals? He would think about all that in the morning.

CHAPTER 30

When Stevo arose the next morning, before putting on his robe, he opened his window curtains to look across to Miss Kara's house. He saw what he was sure was Mr. Brouchard's carriage in front of the patio.

Stevo had never noticed the carriage there so early. He pulled on his trousers, tucking in his shirt as he ran down the stairs two at a time.

Just as he was at the patio, Stevo saw Mr. Brouchard and by the satchel the other man was carrying, Stevo determined him to be a doctor.

Mr. Brouchard saw Stevo and stretched out his hand, saying, "My boy, it is now a matter of time."

Stevo looked to the doctor, who was solemn as he said, "I am afraid Harold is right. I am Doctor Bernard."

To the doctor, Mr. Brouchard said, "This is our very close and good friend, "Steven Markovich."

"How do you do?" said Stevo, looking past the doctor to the house. "May I see Miss Kara, just for a moment?"

"We'll go in with you." said the doctor.

Angel was leaning against a wall, tears streaming down her cheeks. When she saw the men approaching, she pulled up the hem of her apron and wiped her tear-stained face.

Walking past the kitchen, Stevo saw Kate at the table alone, eating her breakfast.

In the semi dark bedroom, Stevo went to Miss Kara's bed. She looked so small and frail, as if her body had shrunk from the evening before. He knelt at her side, taking her small hand in his. She didn't open her eyes, but Stevo could see she was breathing, by the rise and fall of her chest.

Stevo gently kissed her hand, touched her face, and fought back the tears for someone he had, in a sort time, come to admire and care for greatly.

The doctor touched Stevo's shoulder, indicating it was time to leave.

Standing at the carriage, Mr. Brouchard said, "She is hanging on longer than we had expected." He looked at Stevo, "She was waiting for you to come home, my boy. Kara wanted you to have Kate." He grasped Stevo's hand in both of his saying, "There is nothing I won't do for you. Kara asked me to help you make a place for yourself here in New Orleans."

Stevo said, "I have a place." He pointed to the house across the courtyard.

Later, dressed very casually in trousers and a collarless shirt and no hat, Stevo walked the streets of the French Quarter. His thoughts were jumping from Miss Kara to what he, Stevo, would do in New Orleans. He looked at the buildings, the people, the shops, and felt he would find something there. A store window with elegant imported French furniture caught his attention. What if he tried a furniture store here? He did well with the one in Gary. The more he thought about a furniture store, the more he liked it.

Waiting for several carriages and a couple of automobiles to pass, Stevo looked across the street to a three-story building built on a corner surrounded with balconies at all three floors. He thought it an interesting building, an old building with New Orleans charm. Stevo stayed across the street so he could better view the building. As he rounded the corner, he saw that the building extended on the next street. It was as if the building was "V" shaped.

He crossed the street to the double entrance doors of the building. A piece of paper was taped on one of the glass doors reading: CLOSED FOR RENOVATIONS.

Stevo shaded his eyes as he peered through the glass. It had the look of having been closed for a long time. Stevo continued to walk alongside the building until it ended, next to an elegant dress shop.

"Excuse me." said Stevo entering the store. A nicely-dressed attractive lady smiled at him." He asked, "How long has the building next door been closed?"

"How do you do?" said the older lady, her hair coiled fashionably on her head. "The hotel has been closed for several months, much to my disappointment. When it was still receiving guests, I had many customers from there."

"Who owns it?" asked Stevo.

"The owner died leaving it to his widow. I have not seen her in months." said the sales lady. "When she was around, she wasn't very friendly."

"Do you recall her name?" asked Stevo.

"Arnaud." said the lady. "Can I interest you in a nice gift for your lady?"

Stevo gave her a warm smile and shook his head no.

Giving no thought to the fact that his shirt was collarless, with no tie or suit coat, Stevo caught a carriage and hurried to the New Orleans National Bank.

Once in the bank, Stevo could see through the windowed wall that Mr. Brouchard had someone in his office.

Seeing Stevo, the secretary said, "Please sit down, he shouldn't be much longer. I'll see to it that you go in next."

Stevo sat on a comfortable overstuffed chair. There were some magazines and newspapers on a side table. None of these interested him. He fixed his eyes on Mr. Brouchard standing at his desk, talking with someone Stevo could not see. Stevo realized he was nervous when he noticed his knee bouncing up and down.

When the man exited Mr. Brouchard's office, he nodded politely to Stevo who was already standing waiting to be invited in.

Coming through his office door with a folder of papers, Mr. Brouchard saw Stevo. He dropped the folder on his secretary's desk and motioned for Stevo to come into the office.

Without asking to be seated, Stevo plopped into the wooden chair on the opposite side of the desk where Mr. Brouchard sat.

"You look anxious." The banker asked. "Is something the matter? Is it Kara?" His voice sounded almost distressed.

Ignoring the question about Kara, Stevo said, "Tell me about the empty Arnaud building."

"Why do you want to know about that big old building?" asked Mr. Brouchard.

"Tell me if I can buy it." said Stevo, now standing facing the banker with his palms flat on the desk.

Without getting up from his desk, with a wave of his hand, he caught his secretary's attention. She opened the door and looked in.

"Bring me the Arnaud file." he said, "All of it."

Looking at Stevo he again asked, "Why do you want to know about that building? And, why would you want to buy it without having been inside. I know it needs work."

Now Stevo was walking back and forth in front of the desk. He said, "Alright, I want to see the interior. I want to open it up again as a hotel."

Mr. Brouchard, still seated, asked, "What do you know about running a hotel?"

"Nothing," admitted Stevo, but I didn't know anything about the furniture or funeral business and those became successful."

The secretary placed a thick brown folder, tied with brown string on the desk. Mr. Brouchard untied the string and pulled out many papers.

"Arnaud died several months ago." said Mr. Brouchard, looking through the papers. "He failed to sign the insurance papers on the loan. I didn't catch the error until after he died." The banker kept shuffling through the papers, "Because of the debt from the bank for the remodeling, which was never repaid," said Mr. Brouchard, "it appears the bank holds the note on the building." He looked at Stevo, "I think that means we can sell it to you."

Stevo clapped his hands together. "Good. When can we transfer it to me?"

"Wait, my boy!" said Mr. Brouchard. "We will go together and look over the building. You are too anxious and I need to keep you from making what may be a costly mistake."

CHAPTER 31

Two days after Stevo was in Mr. Brouchard's office with questions about the closed hotel, he still had not gotten to see the interior of the building.

Instead, Michael Dukane and Stevo kept watch over Miss Kara's body as she lay in her parlor in a simple casket. The most heartbreaking sight was seeing little Kate look at her mémé, not understanding why she didn't wake up.

On this late, warm August day, the casket was in the back of the black funeral carriage. Behind was an enclosed carriage where Mr. Brouchard and little Kate were seated. Because of his position at the bank, it was best his connection to Miss Kara be kept private. However, many men in town already knew their relationship and many other men also had such arrangements.

Stevo and Dukane walked behind the carriages. Many people Stevo had never seen and people Dukane did not know, walked with them. Stevo assumed most of the people were part of Kara's mixed family. There was no music with the procession. Mr. Brouchard decided against it. He knew it was a celebration of life and death, but he couldn't bear it.

None of Mr. Brouchard's family attended the funeral. At the cemetery, the coffin was carried to the Brouchard mausoleum where a place was already opened. When the coffin was in place, the stone sealing the box had a large elaborately carved letter "K" on it. Her name was not there, nor the date of her birth and passing. Next to it was where, when the time came, Mr. Brouchard would be laid to rest…next to his Kara.

Mr. Brouchard's sister, when she would see the "K" would no doubt know who was behind it, but she was in no position to complain or for that matter, even mention it. Her brother supported both his sister and her daughter, Coralynn.

Not all the mourners came to the house on Canal Street for the funeral luncheon of Gumbo and cake which Virgine and Angel stayed behind to prepare. Angel could not bear to be part of Miss Kara's funeral ceremony. The old woman had been with Kara since Kara was a child of three.

The few that came extended their condolences to Mr. Brouchard, fussed over the confused little Kate, and left after taking some refreshments.

Those that remained made up the close group of Miss Kara's small circle. Stevo had no idea he would be so sad at the loss of Miss Kara, but then, she had been his first true friend in New Orleans. Michael Dukane was visibly distraught. He had felt Kara's love as strongly as he had felt Annette's. Now with the loss of Miss Kara, it was as if he were losing Annette again.

Virgine took little Kate across the courtyard to show her Stevo's house and to distract her from all the sorrow.

Angel closed the door where a black wreath hung, not wanting anyone to come and disturb Mr. Brouchard, who had something he wanted to say. The afternoon being warm, windows were opened to provide a cross draft.

Stevo and Dukane sat at the now cleared dining table. Dukane removed his long, black coat as both Mr. Brouchard and Stevo removed their suit coats.

Angel placed a tray of cold water and a bottle of brandy with proper glasses on the table.

"Sit down, Angel." said Mr. Brouchard. "Here at the table."

His suit coat was draped on the back of the chair. Reaching into the inner pocket, he drew out some papers.

Holding up the papers up for all to see he said, "This is Kara's will."

His voice sounded sad and tired, but he unfolded the first page and began to read, dispensing with the 'I, of sound mind, etc.' He went directly to the disposition of her belongings.

He read, "To my lifelong companion, Angel LaFleur, I leave my pearl earrings and pearl necklace. Also, she may have any of the dresses and stoles she admired. I am leaving her three thousand dollars to buy a cottage near her family and have someone look after her as she has looked after me for all these years.

The little black woman stared open mouthed, dropping her head sobbing. She quickly rose and disappeared into the back of the house.

"To my beloved, Harold Brouchard…" he stopped reading saying, "this isn't relevant." He continued, "Next…to Michael Dukane…" Dukane's eyes widened, he certainly didn't expect anything, in fact he had wondered why he was included at the table.

Mr. Brouchard read, "To Michael Dukane, I leave my gold serpent emerald ring. Whenever he saw the ring, he admired it."

Again going into a pocket of his suit coat, the banker found a black velvet ring box. He handed it to Dukane, who couldn't believe what was happening. He took the ring box, opening the lid. There it was. The gold snake, coiled three times with an emerald on its cobra head.

Dukane removed the ring from the box, slipping it on his finger. It fit his small finger perfectly. With tears in his eyes he said, "I will never remove this ring."

Mr. Brouchard was moved by Dukane's emotion at receiving the ring. The old banker needed to compose himself before continuing.

He had been standing, now he sat, reaching for the brandy. Stevo quickly poured a glass for him. Stevo looked to Dukane, who nodded that he would like some brandy. The three men sipped their brandy in silence.

Stevo showed his pack of cigarettes, his way of asking if he could smoke. When Mr. Brouchard nodded, Stevo offered Dukane a cigarette. Mr. Brouchard reached into his coat for a cigar, for which Stevo promptly supplied a light.

None of the men spoke. They sipped the brandy and smoked in quiet company.

After some moments, still seated, Mr. Brouchard picked up the will and continued reading. "To my beloved granddaughter Kate Brouchard…"

At the name Kate Brouchard, both Stevo and Dukane stared dumbfounded at the banker.

He saw their looks saying, "Yes. I have papers in my bank safe showing that I legally adopted her two years ago." He pointed to his empty brandy glass which was promptly filled by Stevo. "Yes," he continued, "I love Kate and want her to have a name that will get her invited into the homes Kara was denied." He took a good swallow of brandy saying, "Now, back to the will. I leave my house and all my jewelry not already dispensed to Kate, who will be in the care of Steven Markovich until she marries or is an adult."

Now it was Stevo's turn to be surprised. He looked from Mr. Brouchard to Dukane.

Before Stevo could speak, Mr. Brouchard continued, "To Steven Markovich, I have signed over my life insurance. This is my form of payment for the care he has promised to give our beloved Kate. I have every confidence that he will care for her as if she were his own daughter."

The men were silent, thinking about what they had heard and what it meant to the three of them.

Dukane was the first to speak, "Well, Steve. You may be an uncle by blood, but I feel as if this ring," he held his hand out showing the coiled gold snake, "has made me an uncle of sorts. Now we both are bound to look after Kate."

CHAPTER 32

Angel returned to her family in the bayou where she did buy a small rustic cottage.

Virgine was caring for little Kate, who now lived in Stevo's house. The girl's bed, clothes, and toys were brought and set up in the smaller of the two bedrooms at the back of the upper level of the house. Virgine's room was right next to Kate's, where her occasional crying in the night could be heard. That was when Virgine would take Kate into her own larger bed to comfort the child.

Mr. Brouchard was often seen in Kara's house, sitting alone, feeling Kara's ghost near him.

Stevo never intruded when he saw the now very sad and older-looking banker enter the house. From his bedroom window, Stevo could almost feel the sadness and loneliness Mr. Brouchard felt. After all, Stevo knew such pain. He had it when Katya died.

Virgine was much younger than Angel and more of a companion to Kate. They went to the market together, to the parks, watched the street parades, and even played games.

With Stevo's permission, another woman was hired as day help, to clean and do some cooking, freeing Virgine to give all her attention to Kate.

Now more than a week had passed since Stevo spoke to Mr. Brouchard about the closed hotel.

Stevo went to the bank and was immediately shown into Mr. Brouchard's office.

"Hello Steve," he said, not only shaking Stevo's hand, but embracing him. "I know why you are here. Thank you for not insisting we go to Arnaud's place."

Stevo said politely, "I am anxious to get on with my life, but if you aren't ready, I can wait."

Taking an already lit cigar from an ashtray, the tired, older man said, "I remember what it was like to be your age, to want to hurry and get on with my life." He puffed on his cigar, "Now it seems I am only looking back on it. The adventures are all behind me."

With a finger, Stevo smoothed his moustache, saying nothing, waiting for Mr. Brouchard to continue. He watched the old man, who appeared to be having an inner struggle.

Through the windows of his glassed-in office, Mr. Brouchard saw Dukane enter the bank. To Stevo he said, "There's Dukane. Ask him to come in here."

Stevo went into the bank lobby to Dukane, who today, over his black shirt and trousers, wore a long, green coat with yellow fleur-de-lis embroidery.

When Dukane and Stevo entered the office, Mr. Brouchard, with his hat and keys in one hand, shook Dukane's hand with his other hand. He asked, "Michael, are you free to come with us to look at some property?"

With a questioning look to Stevo who was now smiling broadly, he asked, "Where are we going?"

"On an adventure," said Mr. Brouchard as he led them through the lobby and out the doors. "The three of us need a new adventure. One we can accomplish together."

He hailed a motorized cab and the three climbed in.

Along the way, they saw Virgine walking with Kate, coming from the market.

"Stop here," said Stevo, "Let's take Kate with us."

Kate's eyes shone with excitement as she experienced her first ride in a motor vehicle.

Dukane, puzzled, had no idea where they were going or why. And what did Mr. Brouchard mean by 'adventure?'

Michael Dukane's curiosity grew as they stopped at the corner of an empty building. The entrance was on the corner, with the building expanding outward in a V-shape, east and west.

Stevo held Kate's hand as the men stood on the street before the large, three-storied building with iron balconies surrounding each level.

As the three men looked at the building, Mr. Brouchard was concerned; Stevo was excited; Dukane had no idea why they were looking at this monster of a closed building.

Dukane looked with wonder as Mr. Brouchard gave Stevo the keys to the large, arch-shaped wooden doors.

Stevo let go of Kate's hand with which she promptly grasped her grandfather's hand.

The four of them walked in silently, almost reverently, for the lobby was so large, so deserted, so quiet and oh, so full of empty paint cans, scaffolding, and marble floors in need of sweeping and washing.

Dukane was the first to break the awed silence, "Why are we here?"

Mr. Brouchard replied, "Steve wants to buy this hotel and re-open it."

"Oh, merde," said Dukane.

"Well, let's look the place over." said Mr. Brouchard, "The whole place."

With a child's curiosity, Kate let go of her grandfather's hand and skipped ahead, her head full of curls, bouncing with each skip.

"Don't go too far ahead." called Stevo. "Stay where we can see you."

It took them a long time to go through the entire building. Along the tour, Mr. Brouchard gave some information, such as, "There is electricity, which can be turned on along with the running water."

On the lower level they found the huge kitchen and an equally large laundry room. Ascending the staircase to the second level was the large, high-ceilinged ballroom, with a cloak room next to the entry. Here was more remodeling litter to clean up. Each guest room had a door opening onto the balcony.

The last place they looked at was the stone-paved courtyard. Dukane the artist could envision it with statues, pots of flowers, fragrant shade trees, and the fountain, spouting water.

The three men found a bench in the courtyard, sitting to take a rest. They each smoked in silence, contemplating what could be done to resurrect this hotel. Kate found stones to throw into the empty fountain.

"Well," said Stevo, flicking his cigarette ash, "tell me what you think. I feel it could be restored into a beautiful hotel."

Dukane said, "Only half of the rooms were repainted, that would need to be done. What about furniture. I didn't see any."

Mr. Brouchard stood up as if struck. "The furniture!" he exclaimed. "Where is the furniture? It was part of the assets against the remodeling loan."

"Son of a bitch!" he said, surprising his younger companions, who never heard profanity from him. "The furniture belonged to the bank."

"Come, Kate." he called "We are leaving." To Stevo and Dukane he said, "I need to look into this. I need to speak to the bank attorney."

In the lobby stood a tall, brown-haired woman, wearing a long tan lace cotton dress. She had been notified by someone on the street that people were in the building. Behind her was a white servant, wearing what Stevo recognized as a peasant skirt and blouse from the old country.

The woman had a plain but angry face, making her look unattractive. With hands on her hips, she demanded, "What are you people doing in my building? I have sent for the police. You are trespassing."

Mr. Brouchard stepped forward, surprising Mrs. Arnaud, who now recognized him. He asked, "What happened to the furniture?"

She blinked her eyes, saying, "I have no idea what my husband did with the furniture. I knew nothing of his business."

Calmly, the banker said, "The furniture was here when he died. The bank has an inventory of all the assets." He gave her a stern look, "When did you sell everything? Where are the large wall mirrors? We didn't see them during our inspection."

Ignoring his question, Mrs. Arnaud said, "It appears I need to contact my solicitor. You have no right to be here."

"Please do call your solicitor." said Mr. Brouchard, smiling. "You do not own the building. The bank does. When the police come here, I shall have them arrest you for robbery…for the theft of the furnishings."

Mrs. Arnaud could not think of a reply. *She did sell the furnishings.*

Behind Mrs. Arnaud, Stevo saw the white servant holding Kate's hand. She was showing Kate a dance. Step, step, point forward, step back. Again, step, step, point forward. He could see the smile on Kate's face as she tried to keep up with the step, laughing out loud when they came to the hop. Stevo recognized the dance steps as a circle dance, a kolo from the old country.

Mrs. Arnaud turned to leave. She had to get out of there. Noticing Kate and her servant dancing, she said, so all could hear, "Some of the Slavs are dumber than the blacks."

Stevo pushed past Mrs. Arnaud to where Kate and the girl were doing the kolo. To the girl, he asked in Croatian, "Yeli volish Gospa? Do you like the madam?"

"Ne…no." She replied.

"Govorish Engleski? Do you speak English? Stevo asked.

"Da, yes." she said, "I speak English, Croatian, and a little Italian."

Mrs. Arnaud took the girl by the arm, "Come we are leaving."

Stevo removed Mrs. Arnaud's hand from the girl's arm saying, "She is no longer working for you. You not only insulted her, but me when you said Slavs were dumb."

He took Mrs. Arnaud by the arm, leading her out the large, arched doors.

"Do call your solicitor" he said. "We have a lot to settle, dumb Slav that I am."

In the next weeks, Dragitza became Kate's companion. The little girl was happy under the Croatian girl's care. Well, Dragitza wasn't a girl. She was a 24-year-old widow. Her husband had been a fisherman who was washed overboard during a terrible storm while fishing.

Stevo was happy with how the renovations of the hotel were progressing.

Mrs. Arnaud, realizing she had no claim to the building and that she was at fault for selling what she did, signed over to the bank some stock shares she had in order to avoid being arrested.

Mr. Brouchard, who spent much of his time overseeing the renovations, did indeed feel as if he was on a new adventure.

He would join Stevo as often as he could get away from the bank.

He spent much time at the house across from Stevo's. Kara was gone, but he felt comfortable there. When Virgine knew he was there, she brought him meals and sometimes Kate would join him. He especially enjoyed seeing how happy Kate was. The little girl loved going to the waterfront to play with Dragitza's nieces and neighbors. It did not matter that Kate did not speak Croatian, she and the children on the waterfront played hide and seek, tag, or house, understanding each other without words. She often came home in need of a bath or good scrubbing.

Stevo was at the still-unopened hotel almost every day. He watched all the workers, keeping track of what was ordered, hours the men worked, and especially if the jobs were done well.

Michael Dukane was made a consultant. He wanted no pay. So, instead, Stevo and Mr. Brouchard gave him a small partnership.

Mr. Brouchard and Stevo were equal partners, the share being transferred to the survivor in the event of death. Stevo knew that Mr. Brouchard meant for the hotel to be Stevo's alone one day.

Dukane was bursting with good ideas as to the décor. It was not unusual to see him on a ladder in an already painted room, drawing designs over the doorways or around the windows.

On the few occasions Stevo went to the waterfront to bring Kate home, he would stop in at Dragitza's home. He found himself feeling very comfortable and at home in the little cottage. It was always full of familiar smells. Stevo never refused an offer of civapcici or cheese strudel.

He was especially comfortable having a beer or slivovitz at a tavern with Dragitza's brothers, who were fishermen.

Stevo paid Dragitza for taking care of Kate. It was understood that when the hotel was in operation, she would have a full time position there.

Stevo's dreams were mostly about the hotel. He dreamed of the workers, of how the rooms would look, and even the courtyard.

One night, after a late afternoon visit to Dragitza's to take Kate home, he stayed for a meal of sarma. He enjoyed the stuffed cabbage and a beer with one of Dragitza's brothers.

It was on that night Katya and Milan, holding hands, came to Stevo in his dream. He had this dream back in Gary, before he left for New Orleans. In the dream Katya was smiling at him.

He awoke from this dream, sitting up in bed. He remembered before he and Katya married that she had a similar dream. In her dream, her first husband Ivan and the Gypsy Zoltan came to her. They stood smiling at her.

He remembered she had said, "They have set me free."

Did this dream mean that Katya had set him free? Free to perhaps, love again?

CHAPTER 33

The grand opening of the newly-decorated and newly-named Dalmatcia Hotel, after three months of renovations, was a sight to see. People in formal attire came to see the hotel and eat at the restaurant. Stevo named the hotel after the area where he was born.

The lobby had plush seating, beautiful tables with vases of flowers, and violinists in the background playing soft music.

Standing with Stevo, and watching the people arriving Mr. Brouchard said, "Well, my boy, when you said you wanted to reopen the old Arnaud place, I was worried for you. But, now…now that I see what we have here, I am so pleased and proud."

The guest rooms were decorated with a European flair. The ballroom on the second floor had a raised bandstand and a bar with seating away from the dance floor.

A smoking room, for men only, where card playing was allowed, was on the main floor, near the courtyard.

A man Stevo did not know stopped to shake his hand, saying, "Sir, this hotel and the rooms are a pleasure to look at. My friends and I will enjoy visiting the men's smoking room."

Behind the registration desk, above the cubbyholes for mail and keys was a large Dukane portrait. It was of Miss Kara. Many guests seeing the portrait would comment, "Isn't she beautiful? Who do you suppose she is?"

Stevo listened for comments, so far all of them complimentary, from the people as they looked about, walking through the hotel lobby. From the lobby one could enter the now beautiful courtyard, with Roman statues and so many flowers that the scent was almost intoxicating.

Dukane, already well-known for his portraits, had his paintings of New Orleans scenes decorate the walls and the

Miss Kara Restaurant. The restaurant was on its way to becoming famous for its menu of seafood offerings.

On the front of the menu was a copy of the portrait of Kara which was in the lobby. A bit of exaggeration was printed on the back of the menu stating that the selections on the menu were Miss Kara's favorites, personally chosen by her.

The gift shop off the lobby had tasteful gifts, prints of Michael Dukane's New Orleans scenic pictures, and of course, nicely-boxed Pralines and other sweets. There were none of the voodoo dolls or charms one found at the French Market or sold by the street vendors.

Mr. Brouchard looked younger and happy. He discovered that he was not too old for a new adventure. His male friends envied him, his new found energy, and his enthusiasm for the hotel. Several women found him to be a very attractive mature man.

Dukane was getting so many orders for portraits from guests and locals that he seriously thought of hiring artists to finish some already-started portraits, without the buyer's knowledge, of course.

Dragitza worked very hard on improving her English. No longer wearing her old world dress, she now looked fashionably elegant in dresses of the current styles.

Dragitza was pretty, and wore her light brown hair held up with a tortoise shell comb. She worked at the hotel restaurant seating guests in the dining room. She was even proficient enough with her writing that she could register guests or check them out when they were leaving.

Because of the long hours she insisted on working, she had her own room in the hotel. The excitement of working at the Dalmatcia made her happy and it showed in her face and in the sparkle of her eyes.

Virgine brought a very happy Kate to the hotel often, letting the little girl wander about, but never out of her sight.

DESTINY...

Ivanka Babich left her village in Croatia for America, where instead of Stanko Perpich she found a better man and a happy life.

Barbra Vladeslav and Josef Popovich left Zagreb for Gary, Indiana. There they discovered they loved each other. They were given a baby to care for as their own. In time, Dr. Popovich got his certification to practice medicine in America.

Tomo Mandich came to America as an indentured worker. He now owned a successful furniture and funeral business. It would only grow better when he moved from The Patch to the upper Glen Park section of Gary.

Stevo Markovich was drawn to New Orleans by some unknown urge. It brought him fortune and put in his path a woman who might be an ideal wife for him, and a mother to Kate.

What human eyes could not see at the cemetery in Tolleston, were Katya and Milan's spirits walking together hand-in–hand, for the rest of eternity.

These are only some of the things that DESTINY DELIVERED.

THE END

CPSIA information can be obtained
at www.ICGtesting.com
Printed in the USA
LVHW030912021118
595451LV00003B/5/P

9 781634 910040